Praise for Nora Roberts

"Roberts is among the best popular novelists currently at work."
—*The Washington Post*

"The woman can spin a yarn." —*The Dallas Morning News*

"Exciting, romantic, great fun." —*Cosmopolitan*

"Nora Roberts just keeps getting better and better."
—*Milwaukee Journal Sentinel*

"Roberts shines." —*Publishers Weekly* (starred review)

"Her considerable talents at creating richly compelling characters and witty, spellbinding stories come into full bloom in a paranormal-tinged romance." —*Booklist*

"As always, Nora Roberts's characters are superb, the plot is riveting, and the narrative flows like quicksilver ... terrific." —*Affair de Coeur*

"Roberts has always been a winner at sexual tension and sexy dialogue." —*Kirkus Reviews*

Nora Roberts & J. D. Robb

REMEMBER WHEN

Nora Roberts

Series

SPELLBOUND

Nora Roberts

JOVE BOOKS, NEW YORK

THE BERKLEY PUBLISHING GROUP
Published by the Penguin Group
Penguin Group (USA) Inc.
375 Hudson Street, New York, New York 10014, USA

Penguin Group (Canada), 90 Eglinton Avenue East, Suite 700, Toronto, Ontario M4P 2Y3, Canada
(a division of Pearson Penguin Canada Inc.)
Penguin Books Ltd., 80 Strand, London WC2R 0RL, England
Penguin Group Ireland, 25 St. Stephen's Green, Dublin 2, Ireland (a division of Penguin Books Ltd.)
Penguin Group (Australia), 250 Camberwell Road, Camberwell, Victoria 3124, Australia
(a division of Pearson Australia Group Pty. Ltd.)
Penguin Books India Pvt. Ltd., 11 Community Centre, Panchsheel Park, New Delhi—110 017, India
Penguin Group (NZ), Cnr. Airborne and Rosedale Roads, Albany, Auckland 1310, New Zealand
(a division of Pearson New Zealand Ltd.)
Penguin Books (South Africa) (Pty.) Ltd., 24 Sturdee Avenue, Rosebank, Johannesburg 2196,
South Africa

Penguin Books Ltd., Registered Offices: 80 Strand, London WC2R 0RL, England

SPELLBOUND

A Jove Book / published by arrangement with the author

PRINTING HISTORY
Jove mass-market edition / September 2005

"Spellbound" was previously included as a short story in *Once Upon a Castle* published by Jove in March 1998.

ISBN: 0-515-14077-5

JOVE®
Jove Books are published by The Berkley Publishing Group,
a division of Penguin Group (USA) Inc.,
375 Hudson Street, New York, New York 10014.
JOVE is a registered trademark of Penguin Group (USA) Inc.
The "J" design is a trademark belonging to Penguin Group (USA) Inc.

PRINTED IN THE UNITED STATES OF AMERICA

10   9   8   7   6   5   4   3   2

To all my wonderful friends
in this life and all the others

SPELLBOUND

PROLOGUE

Love. My love. Let me into your dreams. Open your heart again and hear me. Calin, I need you so. Don't turn from me now, or all is lost. I am lost. Love. My love.

Calin shifted restlessly in sleep, turned his face into the pillow. Felt her there, somehow. Skin, soft and dewy. Hands, gentle and soothing. Then drifted into dreams of cool and quiet mists, hills of deep, damp green that rolled to forever. And the witchy scent of woman.

The castle rose atop a cliff, silver stone spearing into stormy skies, its base buried in filmy layers of fog that ran like a river. The sound of his mount's bridle jingled battle-bright on the air as he rode, leaving the green hills behind and climbing high on rock. Thunder sounded in the west, over the sea. And echoed in his warrior's heart.

Had she waited for him?

His eyes, gray as the stone of the castle, shifted, scanned, searching rock and mist for any hole where a foe could hide. Even as he urged his mount up the rugged path cleaved into the cliff he knew he carried the stench of war and death, that it had seeped into his pores just as the memories of it had seeped into his brain.

Neither body nor mind would ever be fully clean of it.

His sword hand lay light and ready on the hilt of his weapon. In such places a man did not lower his guard. Here magic stung the air and could embrace or threaten. Here faeries plotted or danced, and witches cast their spells for good or ill.

Atop the lonely cliff, towering above the raging sea, the castle stood, holding its secrets. And no man rode this path without hearing the whispers of old ghosts and new spirits.

Had she waited for him?

The horse's hooves rang musically over the rock until at last they traveled to level ground. He dismounted at the foot of the keep just as lightning cracked the black sky with a blaze of blinding white light.

And she was there, just there, conjured up out of storm-whipped air. Her hair was a firefall over a dove-gray cloak, alabaster skin with the faint bloom of rose, a generous mouth just curved in knowledge. And eyes as blue as a living star and just as filled with power.

His heart leaped, and his blood churned with love, lust, longing.

She came to him, wading through the knee-high mists, her beauty staggering. With his eyes on hers, he swung off his horse, eager for the woman who was witch, and lover.

"Caelan of Farrell, 'tis far you've traveled in the dark of the night. What do you wish of me?"

"Bryna the Wise." His hard, ridged lips bowed in a smile that answered hers. "I wish for everything."

"Only everything?" Her laugh was low and intimate. "Well, that's enough, then. I waited for you."

Then her arms were around him, her mouth lifting to his. He pulled her closer, desperate for the shape of her, wild to have whatever she would offer him, and more.

"I waited for you," she repeated with a catch in her voice as she pressed her face to his shoulder. " 'Twas almost too long this time. His power grows while mine weakens. I can't fight him alone. Alasdair is too strong, his dark forces too greedy. Oh, love. My love, why did you shut me out of your mind, out of your heart?"

He drew her away. The castle was gone—only ruins remained, empty, battle-scarred. They stood in the shadow of what had been, before a small house alive with flowers. The scent of them was everywhere, heady, intoxicating. The woman was still in his arms. And the storm waited to explode.

"The time is short now," she told him. "You must come. Calin, you must come to me. Destiny can't be denied, a spell won't be broken. Without you with me, he'll win."

He shook his head, started to speak, but she lifted a hand to his face. It passed through him as if he were a ghost. Or she was. "I have loved you throughout time." As she spoke, she moved back, the mists flowing around her legs. "I am bound to you, throughout time."

Then lifting her arms, raising palms to the heavens, she closed her eyes. The wind roared in like a lion loosed from a cage, lifted her flaming hair, whipped the cloak around her.

"I have little left," she called over the violence of the storm. "But I can still call up the wind. I can still call to your heart. Don't keep it from me, Calin. Come to me soon. Find me. Or I'm lost."

Then she was gone. Vanished. The earth trembled beneath his feet, the sky howled. And all went silent and still.

He awoke gasping for breath. And reaching out.

CHAPTER 1

"Calin Farrell, you need a vacation."

Cal lifted a shoulder, sipped his coffee, and continued to brood while staring out the kitchen window. He wasn't sure why he'd come here to listen to his mother nag and worry about him, to hear his father whistle as he meticulously tied his fishing flies at the table. But he'd had a deep, driving urge to be in the home of his childhood, to grab an hour or two in the tidy house in Brooklyn Heights. To see his parents.

"Maybe. I'm thinking about it."

"Work too hard," his father said, eyeing his own work critically. "Could come to Montana for a couple of weeks with us. Best fly-fishing in the world. Bring your camera." John Farrell glanced up and smiled. "Call it a sabbatical."

It was tempting. He'd never been the fishing enthusiast his father was, but Montana was beautiful. And big. Cal thought he could lose himself there. And shake off the restlessness. The dreams.

"A couple of weeks in the clean air will do you good." Sylvia Farrell narrowed her eyes as she turned to her son. "You're looking pale and tired, Calin. You need to get out of that city for a while."

Though she'd lived in Brooklyn all of her life, Sylvia still referred to Manhattan as "that city" with light disdain and annoyance.

"I've been thinking about a trip."

"Good." His mother scrubbed at her countertop. They were leaving the next morning, and Sylvia Farrell wouldn't leave a crumb or a mote of dust behind. "You've been working too hard, Calin. Not that we aren't proud of you. After your exhibit last month your father bragged so much that the neighbors started to hide when they saw him coming."

"Not every day a man gets to see his son's photographs in the museum. I liked the nudes especially," he added with a wink.

"You old fool," Sylvia muttered, but her lips twitched. "Well, who'd have thought when we bought you that little camera for Christmas when you were eight that twenty-two years later you'd be rich and famous? But wealth and fame carry a price."

She took her son's face in her hands and studied it with a mother's keen eye. His eyes were shadowed, she noted, his face too thin. She worried for the man she'd raised, and the boy he had been who had always seemed to have . . . something more than the ordinary.

"You're paying it."

"I'm fine." Reading the worry in her eyes, recognizing it, he smiled. "Just not sleeping very well."

There had been other times, Sylvia remembered, that her son had grown pale and hollow-eyed from lack of sleep. She exchanged a quick glance with her husband over Cal's shoulder.

"Have you, ah, seen the doctor?"

"Mom, I'm fine." He knew his voice was too sharp, too defensive. Struggled to lighten it. "I'm perfectly fine."

"Don't nag the boy, Syl." But John studied his son closely also, remembering, as his wife did, the young boy who had talked to shadows, had walked in his sleep, and had dreamed of witches and blood and battle.

"I'm not nagging. I'm mothering." She made herself smile.

"I don't want you to worry. I'm a little stressed-out, that's all." That was all, he thought, determined to make it so. He wasn't different, he wasn't odd. Hadn't the battalion of doctors his parents had taken him to throughout his childhood diagnosed an overdeveloped imagination? And hadn't he finally channeled that into his photography?

He didn't see things that weren't there anymore.

Sylvia nodded, told herself to accept that. "Small wonder. You've been working yourself day and night for the last five years. You need some rest, you need some quiet. And some pampering."

"Montana," John said again. "Couple of weeks of fishing, clean air, and no worries."

"I'm going to Ireland." It came out of Cal's mouth before he'd realized the idea was in his head.

"Ireland?" Sylvia pursed her lips. "Not to work, Calin."

"No, to . . . to see," he said at length. "Just to see."

She nodded, satisfied. A vacation, after all, was a vacation. "That'll be nice. It's supposed to be a restful country. We always meant to go, didn't we, John?"

Her husband grunted his assent. "Going to look up your ancestors, Cal?"

"I might." Since the decision seemed to be made, Cal sipped his coffee again. He was going to look up something, he realized. Or someone.

It was raining when he landed at Shannon Airport. The chilly late-spring rain seemed to suit his mood. He'd slept nearly all the way across the Atlantic. And the dreams had chased him. He went through customs, arranged to rent a car, changed money. All of this was done with the mechanical efficiency of the seasoned traveler. And as he completed the tasks, he tried not to worry, tried not to dwell on the idea that he was having a breakdown of some kind.

He climbed into the rented car, then simply sat in the murky light wondering what to do, where to go. He was thirty, a successful photographer who could name his own price, call his own shots. He still considered it a wild twist of fate that he'd been able to make a living doing something he loved. Using what he saw in a landscape, in a face, in light and shadow and texture, and translating that into a photograph.

It was true that the last few years had been hectic and he'd worked almost nonstop. Even now the trunk of the Volvo he'd rented was loaded with equipment, and his favored Nikon rested in its case on the seat beside him. He couldn't get away from it—didn't want to run away from what he loved.

Suddenly an odd chill raced through him, and he thought, for just a moment, that he heard a woman weeping.

Just the rain, he told himself and scrubbed his hands over his handsome face. It was long, narrow, with the high, strong cheekbones of his Celtic forefathers. His nose was straight, his mouth firm and well formed. It smiled often—or it had until recently.

His eyes were gray—a deep, pure gray without a hint of green or blue. The brows over them were strongly arched and tended to draw together in concentration. His hair was black and thick and flowed over his collar. An artistic touch that a number of women had enjoyed.

Again, until recently.

He brooded over the fact that it had been months since he'd been with a woman—since he'd wanted to. Overwork again? he wondered. A byproduct of stress? Why would he be stressed when his career was advancing by leaps and bounds? He was healthy. He'd had a complete physical only weeks before.

But you didn't tell the doctor about the dreams, did you? he reminded himself. The dreams you can't quite remember when you wake up. The dreams, he admitted, that had pulled him three thousand miles over the ocean.

No, damn it, he hadn't told the doctor. He wasn't going that route again. There had been enough psychiatrists in his youth, poking and prodding into his mind, making him feel foolish, exposed, helpless. He was a grown man now and could handle his own dreams.

If he was having a breakdown, it was a perfectly normal one and could be cured by rest, relaxation, and a change of scene.

That's what he'd come to Ireland for. Only that.

He started the car and began to drive aimlessly.

He'd had dreams before, when he was a boy. Very clear, too realistic dreams. Castles and witches and a woman with tumbling red hair. She'd spoken to him with that lilt of Ireland in her voice. And sometimes she'd spoken in a language he didn't know—but had understood nonetheless.

There'd been a young girl—that same waterfall of hair, the same blue eyes. They'd laughed together in his dreams. Played together—innocent childhood games. He remembered that his parents had been amused when he'd spoken of his friend. They had passed it off, he thought, as the natural imagination of a sociable only child.

But they'd been concerned when he seemed to know things, to see things, to speak of places and people he couldn't have had knowledge of. They'd worried over him when his sleep was disturbed night after night—when he began to walk and talk while glazed in dreams.

So, after the doctors, the therapists, the endless sessions, and those quick, searching looks that adults thought children couldn't interpret, he'd stopped speaking of them.

And as he'd grown older, the young girl had grown as well. Tall and slim and lovely—young breasts, narrow waist, long legs. Feelings and needs for her that weren't so innocent had begun to stir.

It had frightened him, and it had angered him. Until he'd blocked out that soft voice that came in the night. Until he'd turned away from the image that haunted his dreams. Finally, it had stopped. The dreams stopped. The little flickers in his mind that told him where to find lost keys or had him reaching for the phone an instant before it rang ceased.

He was comfortable with reality, Cal told himself. Had chosen it. And would choose it again. He was here only to prove to himself that he was an ordinary man suffering from overwork. He would soak up the atmosphere of Ireland, take the pictures that pleased him. And, if necessary, take the pills his doctor had prescribed to help him sleep undisturbed.

He drove along the storm-battered coast, where wind roared in over the sea and held encroaching summer at bay with chilly breath.

Rain pattered the windshield, and fog slithered over the ground. It was hardly a warm welcome, yet he felt at home. As if something, or someone, was waiting to take him in from the storm. He made himself laugh at that. It was just the pleasure of being in a new place, he decided. It was the anticipation of finding new images to capture on film.

He felt a low-grade urge for coffee, for food, but easily blocked it as he absorbed the scenery. Later, he told himself. He would stop later at some pub or inn, but just now he had to see more of this haunting landscape. So savagely beautiful, so timeless.

And if it was somehow familiar, he could put that down to place memory. After all, his ancestors had roamed these spearing cliffs, these rolling green hills. They had been warriors, he thought. Had once painted themselves blue and screamed out of the forests to terrorize the enemy. Had strapped on armor and hefted sword and pike to defend their land and protect their freedom.

The scene that burst into his mind was viciously clear. The flash of sword crashing, the screams of battle in full power. Wheeling horses, wild-eyed, spurting blood from a severed arm and the agonizing cry of pain as a man crumpled. The burn as steel pierced flesh.

Looking down as the pain bloomed, he saw blood welling on his thigh.

Carrion crows circling in silent patience. The stench of roasting flesh as bodies burned on a pyre, and the hideous and thin cries of dying men waiting for release.

Cal found himself stopped on the side of the road, out of the car, dragging air into his lungs as the rain battered him. Had he blacked out? Was he losing his mind? Trembling he reached down and ran his hand over his jeans. There was no wound, and yet he felt the echoing ache of an old scar he knew wasn't there.

It was happening again. The river of fear that flowed through him froze over and turned his blood to ice. He forced himself to calm down, to think rationally. Jet lag, he decided. Jet lag and stress, that was all. How long since he'd driven out of Shannon? Two hours? Three? He needed to find a place to stay. He needed to eat. He would find some quiet, out-of-the-way bed-and-breakfast, he thought. Somewhere he could rest and ease his mind. And when the storm had passed, he would get his camera and go for a long walk. He could stay for weeks or leave in the morning. He was free, he reminded himself. And that was sane, that was normal.

He climbed back into the car, steadied himself, and drove along the winding coast road.

The ruined castle came into view as he rounded the curve. The keep, he supposed it was, was nearly intact, but walls had been sheared off, making him think of an ancient warrior with scars from many battles. Perched on a stony crag, it shouted with power and defiance despite its tumbled rocks.

Out of the boiling sky, one lance of lightning speared, exploded with light, and stung the air with the smell of ozone.

His blood beat thick, and an ache, purely sexual, began to spread through his belly. On the steering wheel his fingers tightened. He swung onto the narrow, rutted dirt road that led up. He needed a picture of the castle, he told himself. Several studies from different angles. A quick detour—fifteen or twenty minutes—then he would be on his way to that B and B.

It didn't matter that Ireland was dotted with ruins and old castles—he needed this one.

Mists spread at its base like a river. So intent was he on the light and shadows that played on stone, on the texture of the weeds and wildflowers that forced their way through crevices, that he didn't see the cottage until he was nearly upon it.

It made him smile, though he didn't realize it. It was so charming, so unexpected there beside the ancient stones. Inviting, welcoming, it seemed to bloom like the flowers that surrounded it, out of the cliffside as if planted by a loving hand.

It was painted white with bright blue shutters. Smoke trailed up out of the stone chimney, and a sleek black cat napped beside a wooden rocker on the little covered porch.

Someone made a home here, he thought, and tended it.

The light was wrong, he told himself. But he knew he needed to capture this place, this feeling. He would ask whoever lived here if he could come back, do his work.

As he stood in the rain, the cat uncurled lazily, then sat. It watched him out of startlingly blue eyes.

Then she was there—standing in the lashing rain, the mists swirling around her. Though he'd hadn't heard her approach, she was halfway between the tidy cottage and the tumbling stones of the old castle. One hand was lifted to her heart, and her breath was coming fast as if she'd been running.

Her hair was wet, hanging in deep-red ropes over her shoulders, framing a face that might have been carved out of ivory by a master. Her mouth was soft and full and seemed to tremble as it curved into a smile of welcome. Her eyes were star blue and swimming with emotions as powerful as the storm.

"I knew you would come." The cloak she wore flew back as she raced to him. "I waited for you," she said with the musical lilt of Ireland before her mouth crushed his.

CHAPTER 2

There was a moment of blinding, searing joy. Another of dark, primal lust.

Her taste, sharp, potent, soaked into his system as the rain soaked his skin. He was helpless to do anything but absorb it. Her arms were chained around his neck, her slim, curvy body pressed intimately to his, the heat from it seeping through his sodden shirt and into his bones.

And her mouth was as wild and edgy as the sky thundering above them.

It was all terrifyingly familiar.

He brought his hands to her shoulders, torn for a staggering instant as to whether to pull her closer or push her away. In the end he eased back, held her at arm's length.

She was beautiful. She was aroused. And she was, he assured himself, a stranger. He angled his head, determined to handle the situation.

"Well, it's certainly a friendly country."

He saw the flicker in her eyes, the dimming of disappointment, a flash of frustration. But he couldn't know just how deeply that disappointment, that frustration cut into her heart.

He's here, she told herself. He's come. That's what matters most now. "It is, yes." She gave him a smile, let her fingers linger in his hair just another second, then dropped them to her sides. "Welcome to Ireland and the Castle of Secrets."

His gaze shifted toward the ruins. "Is that what it's called?"

"That's the name it carries now." She had to struggle to

keep her eyes from devouring him, every inch, every expression. Instead she offered a hand, as she would have to any wayward traveler. "You've had a long journey. Come, sit by my fire." Her lips curved. "Have some whiskey in your tea."

"You don't know me." He made it a statement rather than a question. Had to.

In answer, she looked up at the sky. "You're wet," she said, "and the wind's cold today. It's enough to have me offer a seat by the hearth." She turned away from him, stepped up onto the porch where the cat stirred itself to wind through her legs. "You've come this far." Her eyes met his again, held. "Will you come into my home, Calin Farrell, and warm yourself?"

He scooped dripping hair out of his face, felt his bones tremble. "How do you know my name?"

"The same way you knew to come here." She picked up the cat, stroked its silky head. Both of them watched him with patient, unblinking blue eyes. "I baked scones fresh this morning. You'll be hungry." With this, she turned and walked inside, leaving him to come or go as he willed.

Part of him wanted to get back in the car, drive away, pretend he'd never seen her or this place. But he climbed onto the porch, pushed the front door open. He needed answers, and it seemed she had at least some of them.

The warmth struck him instantly. Welcoming warmth redolent with the fragrances of bread recently baked, of peat simmering in the hearth, of flowers just picked.

"Make yourself at home." She set the cat on the floor. "I'll see to the tea."

Cal stepped into the tiny parlor and near to the red eye of the fire. There were flowers, he noted, their petals still damp, filling vases on the stone mantel, pots on the table by the window.

A sugan chair sat by the hearth, but he didn't sit. Instead he studied the room with the sharp eye of an artist.

Quiet colors, he thought. Not pale, but soothing in the choice of deep rose and mossy greens. Woven rugs on the polished floors, mirror-bright woods lovingly cared for and smelling lightly of beeswax. Candles everywhere, in varying lengths, standing in holders of glass and silver and stone.

There, by the hearth, a spinning wheel. Surely an antique, he mused as he stepped closer to examine it. Its dark wood gleamed, and beside it sat a straw basket heaped with beautifully dyed wools.

But for the electric lamps and their jewellike shades, the small stereo tucked into a stack of books on a shelf, he might have convinced himself he'd stepped into another century.

Absently he crouched to pet the cat, which was rubbing seductively against his legs. The fur was warm and damp. Real. He hadn't walked into another century, Cal assured himself. Or into a dream. He was going to ask his hostess some very pointed questions, he decided. And he wasn't going anywhere until he was satisfied with the answers.

As she carried the tray back down the short hallway, she berated herself for losing her sense in the storm of emotion, for moving too quickly, saying too much. Expecting too much.

He didn't know her. Oh, that cut through the heart into the soul. But it had been foolish of her to expect him to, when he had blocked out her thoughts, her need for him for more than fifteen years.

She had continued to steal into his dreams when he was unaware, to watch him grow from boy to man as she herself blossomed into womanhood. But pride, and hurt, and love had stopped her from calling to him.

Until there had been no choice.

She'd known it the moment he stepped onto the ground of her own country. And her heart had leaped. Had it been so wrong, and so foolish, to prepare for him? To fill the house with flowers, the kitchen with baking? To bathe herself in oils of her own making, anointing her skin as a bride would on her wedding night?

No. She took a deep breath at the doorway. She had needed to prepare herself for him. Now she must find the right way to prepare him for her—and what they must soon face together.

He was so beautiful, she thought as she watched him stroke

the cat into ecstasy. How many nights had she tossed restlessly in sleep, longing for those long, narrow hands on her?

Oh, just once to feel him touch her.

How many nights had she burned to see his eyes, gray as storm clouds, focused on her as he buried himself deep inside her and gave her his seed?

Oh, just once to join with him, to make those soft, secret sounds in the night.

They were meant to be lovers. This much she believed he would accept. For a man had needs, she knew, and this one was already linked with her physically—no matter that he refused to remember.

But without the love in the act of mating, there would be no joy. And no hope.

She braced herself and stepped into the room. "You've made friends with Hecate, I see." His gaze whipped up to hers, and her hands trembled lightly. Whatever power she still held was nothing compared with one long look from him. "She's shameless around attractive men." She set the tray down. "Won't you sit, Calin, and have some tea?"

"How do you know who I am?"

"I'll explain what I can." Her eyes went dark and turbulent with emotions as they scanned his face. "Do you have no memory of me then? None at all?"

A tumble of red hair that shined like wet fire, a body that moved in perfect harmony with his, a laugh like fog. "I don't know you." He said it sharply, defensively. "I don't know your name."

Her eyes remained dark, but her chin lifted. Here was pride, and power still. "I am Bryna Torrence, descendant of Bryna the Wise and guardian of this place. You're welcome in my home, Calin Farrell, as long as you choose to stay."

She bent to the tray, her movements graceful. She wore a long dress, the color of the mists curling outside the window. It draped her body, flirted with her ankles. Columns of carved silver danced from her ears.

"Why?" He laid a hand on her arm as she lifted the first cup. "Why am I welcome in your home?"

"Perhaps I'm lonely." Her lips curved again, wistfully. "I

am lonely, and it's glad I am for your company." She sat, gestured for him to do the same. "You need a bit of food, Calin, a bit of rest. I can offer you that."

"What I want is an explanation." But he did sit, and because the hot liquid in his cup smelled glorious, he drank. "You said you knew I would come, you knew my name. I want to know how either of those things is possible."

It wasn't permitted to lie to him. Honesty was part of the pledge. But she could evade. "I might have recognized your face. You're a successful and famous man, Calin. Your art has found its way even into my corner of the world. You have such talent," she murmured. "Such vision." She arranged scones on a small plate, offered it. "Such power inside you."

He lifted a brow. There were women who were willing, eager to rock onto their backs for a man who had a hold on fame. He shook his head. "You're no groupie, Bryna. You didn't open the door to me so that you could have a quick bout of sex with a name."

"But others have."

There was a sting of jealousy in her voice. He couldn't have said why, but under the circumstances it amused him. "Which is how I know that's not what this is, not what you are. In any case, you didn't have the time to recognize my face from some magazine or talk show. The light was bad, the rain pouring down."

His brows drew together. He couldn't be dreaming again, hallucinating. The teacup was warm in his hand, the taste of the sweet, whiskey-laced brew in his mouth. "Damn it, you were waiting for me, and I don't understand how."

"I've waited for you all my life." She said it quietly, setting her cup down untouched. "And a millennium before it began." Raising her hands, she laid them on his face. "Your face is the first I remember, before even my own mother's. The ghost of your touch has haunted me every night of my life."

"That's nonsense." He brought a hand up, curled his fingers around her wrist.

"I can't lie to you. It's not in my power. Whatever I say

to you will be truth, whatever you see in me will be real.''
She tried to touch that part of his mind, or his heart, that
might still be open to her. But it was locked away, fiercely
guarded. She took one long breath and accepted. For now.
''You're not ready to know, to hear, to believe.'' Her eyes
softened a little, her fingertips stroking his temples. ''Ah,
Calin, you're tired, and confused. It's rest you're needing
now and ease for your mind. I can help you.''

His vision grayed, and the room swam. He could see nothing but her eyes, dark blue, utterly focused. Her scent swam
into his senses like a drug. ''Stop it.''

''Rest now, love. My love.''

He felt her lips brush his before he slid blissfully into the
dark.

Cal awoke to silence. His mind circled for a moment, like a
bird looking for a place to perch. Something in the tea, he
thought. God, the woman had drugged him. He felt a quick
panic as the theme from Stephen King's *Misery* played in his
head.

Obsessed fan. Kidnapping.

With a jolt, he sat straight up, terrified, reaching for his
foot. Still attached. The black cat, which had been curled on
the edge of the bed, stretched lazily and seemed to snicker.

''Yeah, funny,'' Cal muttered. He let out a long breath
that trailed into a weak laugh. Letting your imagination turn
cartwheels again, Calin, he told himself. Always been a bad
habit of yours.

He ordered himself to calm down, take stock of the situation. And realized he was buck naked.

Surprise ran a swift race with embarrassment as he imagined Bryna undressing him with those lovely tea-serving
hands. And getting him into bed. How in the hell had the
woman carted him into a bedroom?

For that was where he was. It was a small and charming
room with a tiny stone hearth, a glossy bureau. Flowers and
candles again, books tucked into a recessed nook. A doll-size
chair sat near a window that was framed in white lace cur-

tains. Sunlight slipped through them and made lovely and intricate patterns on the dark wood floor.

At the foot of the bed was an old chest with brass fittings. His clothes, clean and dry, were folded neatly on it. At least she didn't expect him to run around in his skin, he decided, and with some relief reached quickly for his jeans.

He felt immediately better once they were zipped, then realized that he felt not just better. He felt wonderful.

Alert, rested, energized. Whatever she'd given him, he concluded, had rocked him into the solid, restful sleep he hadn't experienced in weeks. But he wasn't going to thank her for it, Cal thought grimly as he tugged on his shirt. The woman went way past eccentric—he didn't mind a little eccentricity. But this lady was deluded, and possibly dangerous.

He was going to see to it that she gave him some satisfactory answers, then he was going to leave her to her fairytale cottage and ruined castle and put some miles between them.

He looked in the mirror over the bureau, half expecting to see a beard trailing down to his chest like Rip Van Winkle. But the man who stared back at him hadn't aged. He looked perplexed, annoyed, and, again, rested. The damnedest thing, Cal mused, scooping his hair back.

He found his shoes neatly tucked beside the chest. Putting them on, he found himself studying the patterns the sunlight traced on the floor.

Light. It struck him all at once, had him jumping to his feet again. The rain had stopped. For Christ's sake, how long had he been sleeping?

In two strides he was at the window, yanking back those delicate curtains. Then he stood, spellbound.

The view was stunning. He could see the rugged ground where the ruined castle climbed, make out the glints of mica in the stone where the sun struck. The ground tumbled away toward the road, then the road gave way to wave after rolling wave of green fields, bisected with stone walls, dotted with lolling cattle. Houses were tucked into valleys and on rises, clothes flapped cheerfully on lines. Trees twisted up, bent by the years of resisting the relentless wind off the sea and glossy green with spring.

He saw quite clearly a young boy pedaling his blue bike along one of the narrow trenches of road, a spotted black-and-white dog racing beside him through thick hedgerows.

Home, Cal thought. Home for supper. Ma doesn't like you to be late.

He found himself smiling, and reached down without thinking to raise the window and let in the cool, moist air.

The light. It swelled his artist's heart. No one could have described the light of Ireland to him. It had to be seen, experienced. Like the sheen of a fine pearl, he thought, that makes the air glimmer, go luminous and silky. The sun filtering through layers of clouds had a softness, a majesty he'd never seen anywhere else.

He had to capture it. Now. Immediately. Surely such magic couldn't last. He bolted out of the room, clattered down the short flight of steps, and burst out into the gentle sun with the cat scampering at his heels.

He grabbed the Nikon off the front seat of his car. His hands were quick and competent as he changed lenses. Then swinging his case over his shoulder, he picked his position.

The fairy-tale cottage, he thought, the abundance of flowers. The light. Oh, that light. He framed, calculated and framed again.

CHAPTER 3

Bryna stepped through the arched doorway of the ruin and watched him. Such energy, such concentration. Her lips bowed up. He was happy in his work, in his art. He needed this time, she thought, just as he'd needed those hours of deep, dreamless sleep.

Soon he would have questions again, and she would have to answer. She stepped back inside, wanting to give him his privacy. Alone with her thoughts, she walked to the center of the castle, where flowers grew out of the dirt in a circle thick with blooms. Lifting her face to the light, raising her arms to the sky, she began her chant.

Power tingled in her fingertips, but it was weak. So weak that she wanted to weep in frustration. Once she had known its full strength; now she knew the pain of its decline.

It was ordained, this I know. But here on ground where flowers grow, I call the wind, I call the sun. What was done can be undone. No harm to him shall come through me. As I will, so mote it be.

The wind came, fluttering her hair like gentle fingers. The sun beat warm on her upturned face.

I call the faeries, I call the wise. Use what power you can devise. Hear me speak, though my charms are weak. Cast the circle for my own true love, guard him fast from below, from above. Harm to none, my vow is free. As I will, so mote it be.

The power shimmered, brighter, warmer. She fought to hold it, to absorb what gift was given. She thrust up a hand, the silver of the ring she wore exploding with light as a single narrow beam shot through the layering clouds and struck. The heat of it flowed up her arm, made her want to weep again. This time in gratitude.

She was not yet defenseless.

Cal clicked the shutter again and again. He took nearly a dozen pictures of her. She stood, still as a statue in a perfect circle of flowers. Some odd trick of the wind made it blow her hair away from her glowing face. Some odd trick of the light made it beam down on her in a single perfect diagonal shaft.

She was beautiful, unearthly. Though his heart stumbled when her fingers appeared to explode with light, he continued to circle her and capture her on film.

Then she began to move. Just a sway of her body, rhythmic, sensual. The wind whipped the thin fabric of her dress, then had it clinging to those slim curves. The language she spoke now was familiar from his dreams. With unsteady hands, Cal lowered the camera. It was unsettling enough that he somehow understood the ancient tongue. But he would see beyond the words and into her thoughts as clearly as if they were written on a page.

Protect. Defend. The battle is nearly upon us. Help me. Help him.

There was desperation in her thoughts. And fear. The fear made him want to reach out, soothe her, shield her. He stepped forward and into the circle.

The moment he did, her body jerked. Her eyes opened, fixed on his. She held up a hand quickly before he could touch her. "Not here." Her voice was raw and thick. "Not now. It waits for the moon to fill."

Flowers brushed her knees as she walked out of the circle. The wind that had poured through her hair gentled, died.

"You rested well?" she asked him.

"What the hell is going on here?" His eyes narrowed. "What the hell did you put in my tea?"

"A dollop of Irish. Nothing more." She smiled at his camera. "You've been working. I wondered what you would see here, and need to show."

"Why did you strip me?"

"Your clothes were damp." She blinked once, as she saw his thoughts in his eyes. Then she laughed, low and long with a female richness that stirred his blood. "Oh, Cal, you have a most attractive body. I'll not deny I looked. But in truth, I'm after preferring a man awake and participating when it comes to the matters you're thinking of."

Though furious, he only angled his head. "And would you find it so funny if you'd awakened naked in a strange bed after taking tea with a strange man?"

Her lips pursed, then she let out a breath. "Your point's taken, well taken. I'm sorry for it. I promise you I was thinking only of giving you your ease." Then the humor twinkled again. "Or mostly only of that." She spread her arms. "Would you like to strip me, pay me back in kind?"

He could imagine it, very well. Peeling that long, thin dress away from her, finding her beneath. "I want answers." His voice was sharp, abrupt. "I want them now."

"You do, I know. But are you ready, I wonder?" She turned a slow circle. "Here, I suppose, is the place for it. I'll tell you a story, Calin Farrell. A story of great love, great betrayal. One of passion and greed, of power and lust. One of magic, gained and lost."

"I don't want a story. I want answers."

"It's the same they are. One and the other." She turned back to him, and her voice flowed musically. "Once, long ago, this castle guarded the coast, and its secrets. It rose silver and shining above the sea. Its walls were thick, its fires burned bright. Servants raced up and down the stairways, into chambers. The rushes were clean and sweet on the floor. Magic sang in the air."

She walked toward curving steps, lifted her hem and began to climb. Too curious to argue, Cal followed her.

He could see where the floors had been, the lintels and stone bracings. Carved into the walls were small openings. Too shallow for chambers, he imagined. Storage, perhaps. He saw, too, that some of the stones were blackened, as if from a great fire. Laying a hand on one, he swore he could still feel heat.

"Those who lived here," she continued, "practiced their art and harmed none. When someone from the village came here with ails or worries, help was offered. Babies were born here," she said as she stepped through a doorway and into the sun again. "The old died."

She walked across a wide parapet to a stone rail that stood over the lashing sea.

"Years passed in just this way, season to season, birth to death. It came to be that some who lived here went out into the land. To make new places. Over the hills, into the forests, up into the mountains, where the faeries have always lived."

The view left him thunderstruck, awed, thrilled. But he turned to her, cocked a brow. "Faeries."

She smiled, turned and leaned back against the rail.

"One remained. A woman who knew her fate was here, in this place. She gathered her herbs, cast her spells, spun her wool. And waited. One day he came, riding over the hills on a fine black horse. The man she'd waited for. He was a warrior, brave and strong and true of heart. Standing here, just here, she saw the sun glint off his armor. She prepared for him, lighting the candles and torches to show him the way until the castle burned bright as a flame. He was wounded."

Gently she traced a fingertip on Cal's thigh. He forced himself not to step back, not to think about the hallucination he'd had while driving through the hills toward this place.

"The battle he had fought was fierce. He was weary in body and heart and in mind. She gave him food and ease and the warmth of her fire. And her love. He took the love she gave, offered back his own. They were all to each other from that moment. His name was Caelan, Caelan of Farrell, and hers Bryna. Their hearts were linked."

He stepped back now, dipping his hands into his pockets. "You expect me to buy that?"

"What I offer is free. And there's more of the story yet." The frustration at having him pull back flickered over her face. "Will you hear it, or not?"

"Fine." He moved a shoulder. "Go ahead."

She turned, clamped her hands on the stone balustrade, let

the thunder of the sea pound in her head. She stared down at that endless war of water and rock that fought at the base of the cliff.

"They loved each other, and pledged one to the other. But he was a warrior, and there were more battles to fight. Whenever he would leave her, she watched in the fire she made, saw him wheel his horse through smoke and death, lift his sword for freedom. And always he came back to her, riding over the hills on a fine black horse. She wove him a cloak out of dark gray wool, to match his eyes. And a charm she put on it, for protection in battle."

"So you're saying she was a witch?"

"A witch she was, yes, with the power and art that came down through the blood. And the vow she'd taken to her heart, as close as she'd taken the man she loved, to harm none. Her powers she used only to help and to heal. But not all with power are true. There was one who had chosen a different path. One who used his power for gain and found joy in wielding it like a bloody sword."

She shuddered once, violently, then continued. "This man, Alasdair, lusted for her—for her body, her heart, her soul. For her power as well—for she was strong, was Bryna the Wise. He came into her dreams, creeping like a thief, trying to steal from her what belonged to another. Trying to take what she refused to give. He came into her home, but she would not have him. He was fair of face, his hair gold and his eyes black as the path he'd chosen. He thought to seduce her, but she spurned him."

Her fingers tightened on the stone, and her heart began to trip. "His anger was huge, his vanity deep. He set to kill the man she loved, casting spells, weaving charms of the dark. But the cloak she had woven and the love she had given protected him from harm. But there are more devious ways to destroy. Alasdair used them. Again in dreams he planted seeds of doubt, hints of betrayal in Caelan's sleeping mind. Alasdair gave him visions of Bryna with another, painted pictures of her wrapped in another man's arms, filled with another man's seed. And with these images tormenting his mind, Caelan rode his fine black horse over the hills to this place. And finding her he accused her.

"She was proud," Bryna said after a moment. "She would not deny such lies. They argued bitterly, tempers ruling over hearts. It was then that he struck—Alasdair. He'd waited only for the moment, laughing in the shadows while the lovers hurled pain at each other. When Caelan tore off his cloak, hurled it to the ground at her feet, Alasdair struck him down so that his blood ran through the stones and into the ground."

Tears glinted into her eyes, but went unshed as she faced Calin. "Her grief blinded her, but she cast the circle quickly, fighting to save the man she loved. His wound was mortal and there was no answer for him but death. She knew but refused to accept, and turned to meet Alasdair."

She lifted her voice over the roar of the sea. It came stronger now, this story through her. "Then the walls of this place rang with fury, with magic loosed. She shielded her love and fought like a warrior gone wild. And the sky thundered, clouds dark and thick covered the full white moon and blotted out the stars. The sea thrashed like men pitched in battle and the ground trembled and heaved.

"In the circle, weak and dying, Caelan reached for his sword. But such weapons are useless against witchcraft, light and dark, unless wielded with strength. In his heart he called for her, understanding now his betrayal and his own foolish pride. Her name was on his lips as he died. And when he died, her heart split in two halves and left her defenseless."

She sighed, closed her eyes briefly. "She was lost without him, you see. Alasdair's power spread like vultures' wings. He would have her then, willing or not. But with the last of her strength, she stumbled into the circle where her lover's blood stained the ground. There a vow she made, and a spell she cast. There, while the walls rang and the torches burned, she swore her abiding love for Caelan. For a thousand years she would wait, she would bide. She sent the fire roaring through her home, for she would not let Alasdair have it. And the spell she cast was this."

She drew a deep breath now, kept her eyes on his. "A thousand years to the night, they would come back and face

Alasdair as one. If their hearts were strong, they would defeat him in this place. But such spells have a price, and hers was to vow that if Caelan did not believe, did not stand with her that night as one, her power would wink out. And she would belong to Alasdair. Pledging this, she knelt beside her love, embraced him. And vanished them both.''

He waited a moment, surprised that he'd found her story and the telling of it hypnotic. Studying her, he rocked back on his heels. "A pretty tale, Bryna.''

"Do you still see it as such?'' She shook her head, her eyes pleading. "Can you look at me, hear me, and remember nothing?''

"You want me to believe I'm some sort of reincarnation of a Celtic warrior and you're the reincarnation of a witch.'' He let out a short laugh. "We've waited a millennium and now we're going to do battle with the bad witch of the west? Come on, honey, do I look that gullible?''

She closed her eyes. The telling of the tale, the reliving of it had tired her. She needed all her resources now. "He has to believe,'' she murmured, pacing away from the wall. "There's no time for subtle persuading.'' She whirled back to face him. "You had a vivid imagination as a child,'' she said angrily. "It's a pity you tossed it aside. Tossed me aside—''

"Listen, sweetheart—''

"Oh, don't use those terms with me. Haven't I heard you croon them to other women as you guided them into bed? I didn't expect you to be a monk waiting for this day, but did you have to enjoy it so damn much?''

"Excuse me?''

"Oh, never mind. Just never mind.'' She gestured impatiently as she paced. " 'A pretty tale,' he says. Did it take a millennium to make him so stubborn, so blind? Well, we'll see, Calin Farrell, what we'll see.''

She stopped directly in front of him, her eyes burning with temper, her face flushed with it. "A reincarnation of a witch? Perhaps that's true. But you'll see for yourself one simple fact. I am a witch, and not without power yet.''

"Crazy is what you are.'' He started to turn.

"Hold!" She drew in a breath, and the wind whipped again, wild and wailing. His feet were cemented to the spot. "See," she ordered and flung a hand down toward the ground between them.

It was the first charm learned, the last lost. Though her hand trembled with the effort, the fire erupted, burning cold and bright.

He swore and would have leaped back if he'd been able. There was no wood, there was no match, just that golden ball of flame shimmering at his feet. "What the hell is this?"

"Proof, if you'll take it." Over the flames, she reached out a hand. "I've called to you in the night, Calin, but you wouldn't hear me. But you know me—you know my face, my mind, my heart. Can you look at me and deny it?"

"No." His throat was dust-dry, his temples throbbing. "No, I can't. But I don't want this."

Her hand fell to her side. The fire vanished. "I can't make you want. I can only make you see." She swayed suddenly, surprising them both.

"Hey!" He caught her as her legs buckled.

"I'm just tired." She struggled to find her pride at least, to pull back from him. "Just tired, that's all."

She'd gone deathly pale, he noted, and she felt as limp as if every bone in her body had melted. "This is crazy. This whole thing is insane. I'm probably just having another hallucination."

But he swept her up into his arms and carried her down the circle of stone steps and away from the Castle of Secrets.

CHAPTER 4

"Brandy," he muttered, shouldering open the door to the cottage. The cat slipped in like smoke and led the way down the short hall. "Whiskey. Something."

"No." Though the weakness still fluttered through her, she shook her head. "I'm better now, truly."

"The hell you are." She felt fragile enough to dissolve in his arms. "Have you got a doctor around here?"

"I don't need a doctor." The idea of it made her chuckle a little. "I have what I need in the kitchen."

He turned his head, met her eyes. "Potions? Witch's brews?"

"If you like." Unable to resist, she wound her arms around his neck. "Will you carry me in, Calin? Though I'd prefer it if you carried me upstairs, took me to bed."

Her mouth was close to his, already softly parted in invitation. He felt his muscles quiver. If he was caught in a dream, he mused, it involved all of the senses and was more vivid than any he'd had in childhood.

"I didn't know Irish women were so aggressive. I might have visited here sooner."

"I've waited a long time. I have needs, as anyone."

Deliberately he turned away from the steps and started down the hall. "So, witches like sex."

That chuckle came again, throaty and rich. "Oh, aye, we're fond of it. I could give you more than an ordinary woman. More than you could dream."

He remembered the jolt of that staggering kiss of welcome.

And didn't doubt her word. He made a point of dropping her, abruptly, on one of the two ladder-back chairs at a scrubbed wooden table in the tiny kitchen.

"I dream real good," he said, and she smiled silkily.

"That I know." The air hummed between them before she eased back, tidily folded her hands on the table. "There's a blue bottle in the cupboard there, over the stove. Would you mind fetching it for me, and a glass as well?"

He opened the door she indicated, found the cupboard neatly lined with bottles of all colors and shapes. All were filled with liquids and powders, and none were labeled. "Which one of these did you put in my tea?"

Now she sighed, heavily. "Cal, I put nothing in your tea but the whiskey. I gave you sleep—a small spell, and a harmless one—because you needed it. Two hours only, and did you not wake feeling well and rested?"

He scowled at the bottles, refusing to argue the point. "Which blue one?"

"The cobalt bottle with the long neck."

He set the bottle and a short glass on the table. "Drugs are dangerous."

She poured a careful two fingers of liquid as blue as the bottle that held it. "'Tis herbs." Her eyes flickered up to his, laughed. "And a touch or two of magic. This is for energy and strength." She sipped with apparent enjoyment. "Will you be sitting down, Calin? You could use a meal, and it should be ready by now."

He'd already felt his stomach yearn at the scents filling the room, puffing out of the steam from a pot on the stove.

"What is it?"

"Craibechan." She smiled as his brows drew together. "A kind of soup," she explained. "It's hearty, and your appetite's been off. You've lost more than a pound or two in recent weeks, and I feel the blame for that."

Wanting to see just what craibechan consisted off—and make sure there was no eye of newt or tongue of frog in the mix, he had started to reach for the lid on the pot. Now he drew back, faced her. He was going to make one vital point perfectly clear.

"I don't believe in witches."

A glint of amusement was in her eyes as she pushed back from the table. "We'll set to working on that soon enough."

"But I'm willing to consider some sort of . . . I don't know . . . psychic connection."

"That's a beginning, then." She took out a loaf of brown bread, set it in the oven to warm. "Would you have wine with your meal? There's a bottle you could open. I've chilled it a bit." She opened the refrigerator, took out a bottle.

He accepted it, studied the label. It was his favorite Bourdeax—a wine that he preferred chilled just a bit. Considering, he took the corkscrew she offered.

The obsessed-fan theory just didn't hold, he decided, as he set the open bottle on the slate-gray counter to breathe. No matter how much information she might have dug up about him, she couldn't have predicted he would come to Ireland— and certainly not to this place.

He would accept the oddity of a connection. What else could he call it? It had been her voice echoing through his dreams, her face floating through the mists of his memory. And it had been his hands on the wheel of the car he'd driven up to this place. To her.

It was time, he thought, to discover more about her.

"Bryna."

She paused in the act of spooning stew into thick white bowls. "Aye?"

"How long have you lived here, alone like this?"

"The last five years I've been alone. It was part of the pattern. The wineglasses are to the right of you there."

"How old are you?" He took down two crystal glasses, poured blood-red wine.

"Twenty-six. Four years less than you." She set the bowls on the table, took one of the glasses. "My first memory of you, this time, was of you riding a horse made out of a broom around a parlor with blue curtains. A little black dog chased you. You called him Hero."

She took a sip from her glass, set it down, then turned to take the warmed bread from the oven. "And when he died, fifteen years later on a hot summer day, you buried him in the backyard, and your parents helped you plant a rosebush over his grave. All of you wept, for he'd been very dear. Neither you nor your parents have had a pet since. You don't think you have the heart to lose one again.''

He let out a long, uneasy breath, took a deep gulp of wine. None of that information, none of it, was in his official bio. And certainly none of the emotions were public fare. ''Where is your family?''

''Oh, here and there.'' She bent to give Hecate an affectionate scratch between the ears. ''It's difficult for them just now. There's nothing they can do to help. But I feel them close, and that's comfort enough.''

''So . . . your parents are witches too?''

She heard the amusement in his voice and bristled. ''I'm a hereditary witch. My power and my gift runs through the blood, generation to generation. It's not an avocation I have, Calin, nor is it a hobby or a game. It is my destiny, my legacy and my pride. And don't be insulting me when you're about to eat my food.'' She tossed her head and sat down.

He scratched his chin. ''Yes, ma'am.'' He sat across from her, sniffed at the bowl. ''Smells great.'' He spooned up some, sampled, felt the spicy warmth of it spread through his system. ''Tastes even better.''

''Don't flatter me, either. You're hungry enough to eat a plate of raw horsemeat.''

''Got me there.'' He dug in with relish. ''So, any eye of newt in here?''

Her eyes kindled. ''Very funny.''

''I thought so.'' It was either take the situation with humor or run screaming, he decided. ''Anyway, what do you do up here alone?'' No, he realized, he wasn't sure he wanted to know that. ''I mean, what do you do for a living?''

It was no use being annoyed with him, she told herself. No use at all. ''You're meaning to make money? Well, that's a necessary thing.'' She passed him the bread and salt butter. ''I weave, and sell my wares. Sweaters, rugs, blankets, throws, and the like. It's a soothing art, and a solitary one. It gives me independence.''

''The rugs in the other room? Your work?''

"They are, yes."

"They're beautiful—color, texture, workmanship." Remembering the spinning wheel, he blinked. "Are you telling me you spin your own wool?"

"It's an old and venerable art. One I enjoy."

Most of the women he knew couldn't even sew on a button. He'd never held the lack of domesticity against anyone, but he found the surplus of it intriguing in Bryna. "I wouldn't think a witch would . . . well, I'd think she'd just—you know—*poof.*"

"Proof?" Her brows arched high. "Saying if I wanted a pot of gold I'd just whistle up the wind and coins would drop into my hands?" She leaned forward. Annoyance spiked her voice. "Tell me why you use that camera with all the buttons and business when they make those tidy little things that all but think for you and snap the picture themselves?"

"It's hardly worthwhile if you automate the whole process. If it's to mean anything I have to be involved, in control, do the planning out, see the picture . . ." He trailed off, catching her slow, and smug, smile. "Okay, I get it. If you could just snap your fingers it wouldn't be art."

"It wouldn't. And more, it's a pledge, you see. Not to abuse a gift or take it for granted. And most vital, never to use power to harm. You nearly believe me, Calin."

Stunned that she was right, he jerked back. "Just making conversation," he muttered, then rose to refill his empty bowl, the cat trailing him like a hopeful shadow. "When's the last time you were in the States?"

"I've never been to America." She picked up her wine after he topped it off. "It wasn't permitted for me to contact you, face-to-face, until you came here. It wasn't permitted for you to come until one month before the millennium passed."

Cal drummed his fingers on the table. She sure knew how to stick to a story. "So it's a month to the anniversary of . . . the spell casting."

"No, it's on the solstice. Tomorrow night." She picked up her wine again, but only turned the stem around and around in her fingers.

"Cutting it close, aren't you?"

"You didn't want to hear me—and I waited too long. It was pride. I was wanting you to call to me, just once." Defeated by her own heart, she closed her eyes. "Like some foolish teenage girl waiting by the phone for her boy to call her. You'd hurt me when you turned away from me." Her eyes opened again, pinned him with the sharp edge of her unhappiness. "Why did you turn from me, Calin? Why did you stop answering, stop hearing?"

He couldn't deny it. He was here, and so was she. He'd been pulled to her, and no matter how he struggled to refuse it, he could remember—the soft voice, the plea in it. And those eyes, so incredibly blue, with that same deep hurt glowing in them.

It was, he realized, accept this or accept insanity. "Because I didn't want to answer, and I didn't want to be here." His voice roughened as he shoved the bowl aside. "I wanted to be normal."

"So you rejected me, and the gift you'd been given, for what you see as normality?"

"Do you know what it's like to be different, to be odd?" he tossed back furiously. Then he hissed through his teeth. "I suppose you do," he muttered. "But I hated it, hated seeing how it worried my parents."

"It wasn't meant to be a burden but a joy. It was part of her, part of me that was passed to you, Calin, that small gift of sight. To protect you, not to threaten."

"I didn't want it!" He shoved back from the table. "Where are my rights in all this? Where's my choice?"

She wanted to weep for him, for the small boy who hadn't understood that his uniqueness had been a loving gift. And for the man who would reject it still. "The choice has always been yours."

"Fine. I don't want any of this."

"And me, Calin." She rose as well, slowly, pride in the set of her shoulders, the set of her head. "Do you not want me as well?"

"No." It was a lie, and it burned on his tongue. "I don't want you."

He heard the laughter, a nasty buzz on the air. Hecate hissed, arched her back, then growled out a warning. Cal saw fear leap into Bryna's eyes even as she whirled and flung herself in front of him like a shield.

"No!" Her voice boomed, power and authority. "You are not welcome here. You have no right here."

The shadows in the doorway swirled, coalesced, formed into a man. He wore sorcerer's black, piped with silver, on a slender frame. A face as handsome as a fairy-tale prince was framed with golden hair and accented with eyes as black as midnight.

"Bryna, your time is short." His voice was smooth, laced with dark amusement. "There is no need for this war between us. I offer you such power, such a world. You've only to take my hand, accept."

"Do you think I would? That a thousand years, or ten thousand, would change my heart? Doomed you are, Alasdair, and the choice was your own."

"The wait's nearly at an end." Alasdair lifted a hand, and thunder crashed overhead like swords meeting. "Send him away and I will allow it. My word to you, Bryna. Send him away and he goes unharmed by me. If he stays, his end will be as it was before, and I will have you, Bryna, unbound or in chains. That choice is your own."

She lifted a hand, and light glinted off her ring of carved silver. "Come into my circle now, Alasdair." Her lips curved in a sultry dare, though her heart was pounding in terror, for she was not ready to meet him power to power. "Do you risk it?"

His lips thinned in a sneer, his dark eyes glittering with malicious promise. "On the solstice, Bryna." His gaze flickered to Cal, amusement shining dark. "You, warrior, remember death."

There was pain, bright and sharp and sudden, stabbing into Cal's belly. It burned through him like acid, cutting off his breath, weakening his knees, even as he gripped Bryna's shoulders and shoved her behind him.

"Touch her and die." He felt the words rise in his throat,

heard them come through his lips. He felt the sweat pearl cold and clammy on his brow as he faced down the image.

And so it faded, leaving only a dark glint like a smudge, and an echo of taunting laughter.

CHAPTER 5

Cal pressed a hand to his stomach, half expecting to find blood, and worse, dripping through his fingers. The pain had dulled to numbness, with a slick echo of agony.

"He can't harm you." Bryna's voice registered dimly, made him aware that he was still gripping her arm. "He can only make you remember, deceive you with the pain. It's all tricks and lies with him."

"I saw him." Dazed, Cal studied his own fingers. "I saw it."

"Aye. He's stronger than I'd believed, and more rash, to come here like this." Gently she put a hand over the one bruising her arm. "Alasdair is sly and full of lies. You must remember that, Calin. You must never forget it."

"I saw him," Cal repeated, struggling to absorb the impossible into reality. "I could see through him, the table in the hall, the flowers on it."

"He wouldn't dare risk coming here in full form. Not as yet. Calin, you're hurting my arm."

His fingers jerked, dropped. "Sorry. I lost my head. Seeing ghosts does that to me."

"A ghost he isn't. But a witch, one who embraced the dark and closed out the light. One who broke every oath."

"Is he a man?" He whirled on her so abruptly that she caught her breath, then winced as his hands gripped her arms again. "He looked at you as a man would, with desire."

"We're not spirits. We have our needs, our weaknesses. He wants me, yes. He has broken into my dreams and shown me just what he wants from me. And rape in dreams is no less a rape.'' She trembled and her eyes went blind. For a moment she was only a woman, with a woman's fears. "He frightens me. Is that enough for you? Is it enough that I'd rather die than have his hands on me? He frightens me,'' she said again and pressed her face into Cal's shoulder. "Oh, Calin, his hands are cold, so cold.''

"He won't touch you.'' The need to protect was too strong to deny. His arms tightened, brought her close. "He won't touch you. Bryna.'' His lips brushed over her hair, down her temple. Found hers. "Bryna,'' he said again. "Sweet God.''

She melted into him, yielding like wax, giving like glory. All the confusion, the doubt, the fear slid away from him. Here was the woman, the only, the ever. His hands dived into her hair, fisted in those soft ropes of red silk, pulled her head back so that he could drive the kiss deeper.

Whatever had brought him here he would face. Whatever else he might continue to deny, there was no denying this. Need could be stronger than reason.

The sounds humming in her throat were both plea and seduction. Her heart hammered fast and hard against his, and her body shuddered lightly. She nipped at his lip, urging him on. He heard her sigh his name, moan it, then whisper words ripe with longing.

The words were in Gaelic, and that was what stopped him. He understood them as if he'd been speaking the language all his life.

"Love,'' she had said. "My love.''

"Is this the answer?'' The fury returned as he pushed her back against the wall. "Is this what you want?'' Now his kiss tasted of violence, of desperation, nearly of punishment.

Her own fears sprang hot to her throat, taunting her to fight him, to reject the anger. But she offered no struggle, took the heat, the rough hands until he drew back and stared at her out of stormy eyes.

She took a steadying breath, waited until she was sure her voice would be strong and sure. "It's one answer. Yes, I want you.'' Slowly she unfastened the buttons running down the front of her dress. "I want you to touch me, to take me.''

Parted the material, let it slide to the floor so that she stood
before him defenseless and naked. "Where you like, when
you like, how you like."

He kept his eyes on hers. "You said that to me before,
once before."

Emotions swirling, she closed her eyes, then opened them
again. And smiled. "I did. A thousand years ago. More or
less."

He remembered. She had stood facing him, flowers bloom-
ing at her feet. And she had undraped herself so that the
pearly light had gleamed on her skin. She had offered herself
without restrictions. He'd lost himself in her, flowers crushed
and fragrant under their eager bodies.

He shook his head, and the image faded away. Memory
or imagination, it no longer mattered. He knew only one vital
thing. "This is now. This is you and me. Nothing else
touches it. Whatever happened or didn't happen before, this
is for us."

He scooped her into his arms. "That's the way I want it,"
he stated.

She stared at him, for she was spellbound now. She'd
thought he would simply take her where they stood, seeking
release, even oblivion. She'd tasted the sharp edge of his
passion, felt the violence simmering under his skin. Instead,
he carried her in his arms as if she were something he could
cherish.

And when he laid her on the bed, stepped back to look at
her, she felt a flush warm her cheeks. She managed a quick
smile. "You'll be needing your clothes off," she said, tried
to laugh and sit up, but he touched a hand to her shoulder.

"I'll do it. Lie back, Bryna. I want to see you with your
hair burning over the pillows, and the sun on your skin." He
would photograph her like this, he realized. Would be com-
pelled to see if he could capture the magic of it, of her—
long limbs, slender curves, eyes full of needs and nerves.

He watched her as he undressed, and his voice was quiet
and serious when he spoke. "Are you afraid of me?"

"I wasn't. I didn't expect to be." But her heart was fluttering like bird's wings. "I suppose I am, yes. A little. Because it means . . . everything."

He tossed his clothes toward the little chair, never taking his eyes from hers. "I don't know what I believe, what I can accept. Except one thing." He lowered himself to her, kept his mouth a whisper from hers. "This matters. Here. Now. You. It matters."

"Love me." She drew his mouth down to hers. "I've ached for you so long."

It was slow and testing and sweet. Sighs and secrets, tastes and textures. He knew how her mouth would fit against his, knew the erotic slide of her tongue, the suggestive arch of her hips. He swallowed each catchy breath as he took his hands slowly, so slowly over her. Skimming curves, warming flesh. He filled his hands with her breasts, then his mouth, teasing her nipples with tongue and teeth until she groaned out his name like a prayer.

She took her hands over him, testing those muscles, tracing the small scars. Not a warrior's body, but a man's, she thought. And for now, hers. Her heart beat slow and thick as he used his mouth on her with a patience and concentration she knew now she'd been foolish not to expect.

Her heart beat thickly, the sun warmed her closed lids as pleasure swamped her. And love held so long in her heart bloomed like wild roses.

"Calin."

His name shuddered through her lips when he cupped her. He watched her eyes fly open, saw the deep-blue irises go glassy and blind in speechless arousal. He sent her over the edge, viciously delighted when she cried out, shuddered, when her hands fell weakly.

His, was all he could think as he blazed a hot trail down her thigh. His. His.

Blood thundered in his head as he slipped inside her, as she moaned in pleasure, arched in welcome. Now her eyes were open, vivid blue and intense. Now her arms were around him, a circle of possession. She mated with him, their rhythm ancient and sure.

His strokes went deep, deeper, and his mouth crushed

down on hers in breathless, mutual pleasure. She flew, as she had waited a lifetime to fly, as he emptied himself into her.

She held him close as the tension drained from his body. Stroked his hair as he rested his head between her breasts. "It's new," she said quietly. "Ours. I didn't know it could be. Knowing so much, yet this I never knew."

He shifted, lifted his head so that he could see her face. Her skin was soft, dewy, her eyes slumberous, her mouth rosy and swollen. "None of this should be possible." He cupped a hand under her chin, turned her profile just slightly, already seeing it in frame, in just that light. Black and white. And he would title it *Aftermath*. "I'm probably having a breakdown."

Her laugh was a quick, silly snort. Carefree, careless. "Well, your engine seemed to be running fine, Calin, if you're after asking me."

His mouth twitched in response. "We're pushing into the twenty-first century. I have a fax built into my car phone, a computer in my office that does everything but make my bed, and I'm supposed to believe I've just made love to a witch. A witch who makes fire burn out of thin air, calls up winds where there isn't a breeze in sight."

She combed her fingers through his hair as she'd dreamed of doing countless times. "Magic and technology aren't mutually exclusive. It's only that the second so rarely takes the first into account. Normality is only in the perspective." She watched his eyes cloud at that. "You had visions, Calin. As a child you had them."

"And I put away childish things."

"Visions? Childish?" Her eyes snapped once, then she closed them on a sigh. "Why must you think so? A child's mind and heart are perhaps more open to such matters. But you saw and you felt and you knew things that others didn't. It was a gift you were given."

"I'm no witch."

"No, that only makes the gift more special. Calin—"

"No." He sat up, shaking his head. "It's too much. Let it be for a while. I don't know what I feel." He scrubbed his hands over his face, into his hair. "All I know is that here was where I had to be—and you're who I had to be with. Let the rest alone for a while.''

They had so little time. She nearly said it before she stopped herself. If time was so short, then what they had was precious. If she was damned for taking it for only the two of them, then she was damned.

"Then let it rest we will." She lay back, stretched out a hand for his. "Come kiss me again. Come lie with me."

He skimmed a hand up her thigh, watched her smile bloom slow. And the light. Oh, the light. "Stay right there." He bounded out of bed, grabbing his jeans on the run.

She blinked. "What? Where are you going?"

"Be right back. Don't move. Stay right there."

She huffed out a breath at the ceiling. Then her face softened again and she stretched her arms high. Oh, she felt well loved. Like a cat thoroughly stroked. Chuckling, she glanced over at Hecate, curled in front of the hearth and watching her.

"Aye, you know the feeling, don't you? Well, I like it." The cat only stared, unblinking. Ten seconds. Twenty. Bryna closed her eyes. "I need the time. Damn it, we need it. A few hours after so many years. Why should we be denied it? Why must there be a price for every joy? Go then, leave me be. If the fare comes due, I'll pay it freely."

With a swish of her tail, the cat rose and padded out of the room. Calin's footsteps sounded on the steps seconds later. Prepared to smile, Bryna widened her eyes instead. He'd snapped two quick pictures before she could push herself up and cross her arms over her breast.

"What do you think you're about? Taking photographs of me without my clothes. Put it away. You won't be hanging me on some art gallery wall."

"You're beautiful." He circled the bed, changing angles. "A masterpiece. Drop your left shoulder just a little."

"I'll do no such thing. It's outrageous." Shocked to the core, she tugged at the rumpled spread, pulled it up—and to Cal's mind succeeded only in looking more alluring and rumpled.

But he lowered the camera. "I thought witches were supposed to like to dance naked under the full moon.''

"Going skyclad isn't an exhibition. And there's a time and place for such things. No one snaps pictures of private matters nor of rituals.''

"Bryna.'' Using all his charm, he stepped closer, tugged gently at the sheet she'd pulled over her breasts. "You have a beautiful body, your coloring is exquisite, and the light in here is perfect. Unbelievable.'' He skimmed the back of his fingers over her nipple, felt her tremble. "I'll show them to you first.''

She barely felt the sheet slip to her waist. "I know what I look like.''

"You don't know how I see you. But I'll show you. Lie back for me. Relax.'' Murmuring, he spread her hair over the pillows as he wanted it. "No, don't cover yourself. Just look at me.'' He shot straight down, then moved back. "Turn your head, just a little. I'm touching you. Imagine my hands on you, moving over you. There. And there.'' He braced a knee on the foot of the bed, working quickly. "If I had a darkroom handy, I'd develop these tonight and you'd see what I see.''

"I have one.'' Her voice was breathless, aroused.

"What?''

"I had one put in for you, off the kitchen.'' Her smile was hesitant when he lowered the camera and stared at her. "I knew you would come, and I wanted you to have what you needed, what would make you comfortable.''

So you would stay with me, she thought, but didn't say it.

"You put in a darkroom? Here?''

"Aye, I did.''

With a laugh, he shook his head. "Amazing. Absolutely amazing.'' Rising, he set the camera down on the bureau. "I think you need to be a little more . . . mussed before I shoot the rest of that roll.'' He climbed onto the bed. "The things I do for my art,'' he murmured and covered her laughing mouth with his.

CHAPTER 6

Later, in the breezy evening when the sun gilded the sky and polished the air, he walked with her toward the cliffs. Both his mind and his body were relaxed, limber.

Logically he knew he should be racing to the nearest psychiatric ward for a full workup. But a lonely cliffside, a ruined castle, a beautiful woman who claimed to be a witch—visions and sex and legends. It was a time and place to set logic aside, at least for a while.

"It's a beautiful country," he commented. "I'm still trying to adjust that I've only been here since this morning. Barely twelve hours."

"Your heart's been here longer." It was so simple to walk with him, fingers linked. So simple. So ordinary. So miraculous. "Tell me about New York. All the movies, the pictures I've seen have only made me wonder more. Is it like that, really? So fast and crowded and exciting?"

"It can be." And at that moment it seemed a world away. A thousand years away.

"And your house?"

"It's an apartment. It looks out over the park. I wanted a big space so I could have my studio right there. It's got good light."

"You like to stand on the balcony," she began, then rolled her eyes when he shot her a quick look. "I've peeked now and then."

"Peeked." He caught her chin in his hand before she could turn away. "At what? Exactly?"

"I wanted to see how you lived, how you worked."

She eased away and walked along the rocks, where the water spewed up, showered like diamonds in the sunlight. Then she turned her head, tilting it in an eerily feline movement.

"You've had a lot of women, Calin Farrell—coming and going at all hours in all manner of dress. And undress."

He hunched his shoulders as if he had an itch he couldn't scratch. "You watched me with other women?"

"I peeked," she corrected primly. "And never watched for long in any case. But it seemed to me that you often chose women who were lacking in the area of intelligence."

He ran his tongue around his teeth. "Did it?"

"Well . . ." A shrug, dismissing. "Well, so it seemed." Bending, she plucked a wildflower that had forced its way through a split in the rock. Twirled it gaily under her nose. "Is it worrying you that I know of them?"

He hooked his thumbs in his pockets. "Not particularly."

"That's fine, then. Now, if I were the vindictive sort, I might turn you into an ass. Just for a short time."

"An ass?"

"Just for a short time."

"Can you do that sort of thing?" He realized when he asked it that he was ready to believe anything.

She laughed, the sound carrying rich music over wind and sea. "If I were the vindictive sort." She walked to him, handed him the flower, then smiled when he tucked it into her hair. "But I think you'd look darling with long ears and a tail."

"I'd just as soon keep my anatomy as it is. What else did you . . . peek at?"

"Oh, this and that, here and there." She linked her fingers with his and walked again. "I watched you work in your darkroom—the little one in the house where you grew up. Your parents were so proud of you. Startled by your talent, but very proud. I saw your first exhibition, at that odd wee gallery where everyone wore black—like at a wake."

"SoHo," he murmured. "Christ, that was nearly ten years ago."

"You've done brilliant things since. I could look through your eyes when I looked at your pictures. And felt close to you."

The thought came abruptly, stunning him. He turned her quickly to face him, stared hard into her eyes. "You didn't have anything to do with . . . you haven't made what I can do?"

"Oh, Calin, no." She lifted her hands to cover the ones on her shoulders. "No, I promise you. It's yours. From you. You mustn't doubt it," she said, sensing that he did. "I can tell you nothing that isn't true. I'm bound by that. On my oath, everything you've accomplished is yours alone."

"All right." He rubbed his hands up and down her arms absently. "You're shivering. Are you cold?"

"I was for a moment." Bone-deep, harrowing. Alasdair. She cast it out, gripped his hand tightly and led him over the gentle slope of the hill. "Even as a child I would come here and stand and look out." Content again, she leaned her head against his shoulder, scanning hill and valley, the bright flash of river, the dark shadows cast by twisted trees. "To Ireland spread out before me, green and gold. A dreaming place."

"Ireland, or this spot?"

"Both. We're proud of our dreamers here. I would show you Ireland, Calin. The bank where the columbine grows, the pub where a story is always waiting to be told, the narrow lane flanked close with hedges that bloom with red fuchsia. The simple Ireland."

Tossing her hair back, she turned to him. "And more. I would show you more. The circle of stones where power sleeps, the quiet hillock where the faeries dance of an evening, the high cliff where a wizard once ruled. I would give it to you, if you'd take it."

"And what would you take in return, Bryna?"

"That's for you to say." She felt the chill again. The warning. "Now I have something else to show you, Calin." She glanced uneasily over her shoulder, toward the ruins. Shivered. "He's close," she whispered. "And watching. Come into the house."

He held her back. He was beginning to see that he had run

from a good many things in his life. Too many things. "Isn't it better to face him now, be done with it?"

"You can't choose the time. It's already set." She gripped his hand, pulled. "Please. Into the house."

Reluctantly, Cal went with her. "Look, Bryna, it seems to me that a bully's a bully whatever else he might be. The longer you duck a bully, the worse he gets. Believe me, I've dealt with my share."

"Oh, aye, and had a fine bloody nose, as I remember, from one. The two of you, pounding on each other on the street corner. Like hoodlums."

"Hey, he started it. He tried to shake me down once too often, so I . . ." Cal trailed off, blew out a long breath. "Whoa. Too weird. I haven't thought about Henry Belinski in twenty years. Anyway, he may have bloodied my nose, but I broke his."

"Oh, and you're proud of that, are you now? Breaking the nose of an eight-year-old boy."

"*I* was eight too." He realized that she had maneuvered him neatly into the house, turned the subject, and gotten her own way. "Very clever, Bryna. I don't see that you need magic when you can twist a conversation around like that."

"Just a small talent." She smiled and touched his cheek. "I was glad you broke his nose. I wanted to turn him into a toad—I had already started the charm when you dealt with it yourself."

"A toad?" He couldn't help it, the grin just popped out. "Really?"

"It would have been wrong. But I was only four, and such things are forgiven in the child." Then her smile faded, and her eyes went dark. "Alasdair is no child, Calin. He wants more than to wound your pride, skin your knees. Don't take him lightly."

Then she stepped back, lifting both hands. *I call the wind around my house to swirl.* She twisted a wrist and brought the wind howling against the windows. *Fists of fog against my windows curl. Deafen his ears and blind his eyes. Come aid me with this disguise. Help me guard what was trusted to me. As I will, so mote it be.*

He'd stepped back from her, gaping. Fog crawled over the windows, the wind howled like wolves. The woman before him glowed like a candle, shimmering with a power he couldn't understand. The fire she'd made out of air was nothing compared with this.

"How much am I supposed to believe? Accept?"

She lowered her hands slowly. "Only what you will. The choice will always be yours, Calin. Will you come with me and see what I would show you?"

"Fine." He blew out a breath. "And after, if you don't mind, I'd like a glass of that Irish of yours. Straight up."

She managed a small smile. "Then you'll have it. Come." As she started toward the stairs, she chose her words carefully. "We have little time. He'll work to break the spell. His pride will demand it, and my powers are more . . . limited than they were."

"Why?"

"It's part of it," was all she would say. "And so is what I have to show you. It isn't just me he wants, you see. He wants everything I have. And he wants the most precious treasure of the Castle of Secrets."

She stopped in front of a door, thick with carving. There was no knob, no lock, just glossy wood and that ornate pattern on it that resembled ancient writing. "This room is barred to him by power greater than mine." She passed a hand over the wood, and slowly, soundlessly, the door crept open.

" 'Open locks,' " Cal murmured, " 'whoever knocks.' "

"No, only I. And now you." She stepped inside, and after a brief hesitation, he crossed the threshold behind her.

Instantly the room filled with the light of a hundred candles. Their flames burned straight and true, illuminating a small, windowless chamber. The walls were wood, thickly carved like the door, the ceiling low, nearly brushing the top of his head.

"A humble place for such a thing," Bryna murmured.

He saw nothing but a simple wooden pedestal standing in a white circle in the center of the room. Atop the column was a globe, clear as glass.

"A crystal ball?"

Saying nothing, she crossed the room. "Come closer." She waited, kept her hands at her side until he'd walked up and put the globe between them.

"Alasdair lusts for me, envies you, and covets this. For all his power, for all his trickery, he has never gained what he craves the most. This has been guarded by a member of my blood since before time. Believe me, Calin, wizards walked this land while men without vision still huddled in caves, fearing the night. And this ancient ball was conjured by one of my blood and passed down generation to generation. Bryna the Wise held this in her hands a thousand years past and through her power, and her love, concealed it from Alasdair at the last. And so it remained hidden. No one outside my blood has cast eyes on it since."

Gently, she lifted the globe from its perch, raised it high above her head. Candlelight flickered over it, into it, seemed to trap itself inside until the ball burned bright. When she lowered it, it glowed still, colors dazzling, pulsing, beating.

"Look, my love." Bryna opened her hand so that the globe rolled to her fingertips, clung there in defiance of gravity. "Look, and see."

He couldn't stop his hands from reaching out, cupping it. Its surface was smooth, almost silky, and warmed in his hands like flesh. The pulse of it, the life of it, seemed to swim up his arms.

Colors shifted. The bright clouds they formed parted, a magic sea. He saw dragons spewing fire and a silver sword cleaving through scales. A man bedding a woman in a flower-strewn meadow under a bright white sun. A farmer plowing a rocky field behind swaybacked horses. A babe suckling at his mother's breast.

On and on it went, image after image in a blur of life. Dark oceans, wild stars, a quiet village as still as a photograph. An old woman's face, ravaged with tears. A small boy sleeping under the shade of a chestnut tree.

And even when the images faded into color and light, the power sang. It flooded him, a river of wine. Cool and clean.

It hummed still when the globe was clear again, tossing the flames of the candles into his eyes.

"It's the world." Cal's voice was soft and thick. "Here in my hands."

"The heart of it. The hope for it. Power gleams there. In your hands now."

"Why?" He lifted his gaze to hers. "Why in my hands, Bryna?"

"I am the guardian of this place. My heart is in there as well." She took a slow breath. "I am in your hands, Calin Farrell."

"I can refuse?"

"Aye. The choice is yours."

"And if he—Alasdair—claims this?"

She would stop him. It would cost her life, but she would stop him. "Power can be twisted, abused—but what is used will turn on the abuser, ten times ten."

"And if he claims you?"

"I will be bound to him, a thousand years of bondage. A spell that cannot be broken." But with death, she thought. Only with death. "He is wicked, but not without weaknesses." She laid her hand on the globe so that they held it together. "He will not have this, Calin. Nor will he bring harm to you. That is my oath."

She stared hard into his eyes, murmuring. His vision blurred, his head spun. He lifted a hand as if to push back what he couldn't see. "No."

"To protect." She laid a hand on his cheek as she cast the charm. "My love."

He blinked, shook his head. For a moment his mind remained blank with some faint echo of words. "I'm sorry. What?"

Her lips curved. He would remember nothing, she knew. It was all she could do for him. "I said we need to go." She placed the globe back on the pedestal. "We're not to speak of this outside this room." She walked toward the door, held out a hand. "Come. I'll pour you that whiskey."

CHAPTER 7

That night his dreams were restful, lovely. Bryna had seen to that.

There was a man astride a gleaming black horse, riding hard over hills, splashing through a bright slash of river, his gray cape billowing in a brisk and icy wind.

There was the witch who waited for him in a silver castle atop a spearing cliff where candles and torches burned gold.

There was a globe of crystal, clear as water, where the world swam from decade to decade, century past century.

There was love sweet as honey and need sharp as honed steel.

And when he turned to her in the night, lost in dreams, she opened for him, took him in.

Bryna didn't sleep, nor did she dream. She lay in the circle of his arms while the white moon rose and the shudders his hands had caused quieted.

Who had loved her? she wondered. Cal, or Caelan? She turned her face into his shoulder, seeking comfort, a harbor from fear on this last night before she would face her fate.

He would be safe, she thought, laying a hand over his heart. She had taken great pains, at great risk, to assure it. And her safety depended on the heart that beat quietly under her palm. If he did not choose to give it freely, to stand with her linked by love, she was lost.

So it had been ordained in fire and in blood, on that terrible night a millennium before.

For a thousand years we sleep, a hundred years times ten.

*But blood stays true and hearts are strong when we are born
again. And in this place we meet, with love our lifted shield.
In the shortest night the battle will rage and our destiny be
revealed. My warrior's heart his gift to me, his sword bright
as the moon. If he brings both here of his own free will, we
will bring to Alasdair his doom. When the dawn breaks that
longest day and his love has found a way, our lives will then
be free of thee. As I will, so mote it be.*

The words of Bryna the Wise, lifted high the blazing castle
walls, echoed in her head, beat in her heart. When the moon
rose again, it would be settled.

Bryna lay in the circle of Cal's arms, listened to the wind
whisper, and slept not at all.

When Cal woke, he was alone, and the sun was streaming.
For a moment, he thought it had all been a dream. The
woman—the witch—the ruined castle and tiny cottage. The
globe that held the world. A hallucination brought on, he
thought, by fatigue and stress and the breakdown he'd se-
cretly worried about.

But he recognized the room—the flowers still fresh in the
vases, the scent of them, and Bryna, on the air. True, then.
He pressed his fingers to his eyes to rub away sleep. All true,
and all unbelievable. And all somehow wonderful.

He got out of bed, walked into the charming little bathroom, stepped into the clawfoot tub, and twitched the circling
curtain into place. He adjusted the shower for hot and let the
steam rise.

He hadn't showered with her yet, Cal thought, grinning as
he turned his face into the spray. Hadn't soaped that long,
lovely body of hers until it was slick and slippery, hadn't
seen the water run through that glorious mane of flame-red
hair. Had yet to ease inside her while the water ran hot and
the steam rose in clouds.

His grin winked off, replaced by a look of puzzlement.
Had he turned to her in the night, in his dreams, seeking that
tangle of tongues and limbs, that slow, satiny slide of bodies?

Why couldn't he remember? Why couldn't he be sure?

What did it matter? Annoyed with himself, he flicked off

the water, snatched a towel from the heating rack. Whether it had been real or a dream, she was there for him as he'd wanted no one to be before.

Was it you, or another, she moved under in the night?

Cal's eyes went dark as the voice whispered slyly in his head. He toweled off roughly.

She uses you. Uses you to gain her own ends. Spellbinds you until she has what she seeks.

The room was suddenly airless, the steam thick and clogging his lungs. He reached blindly for the door, found only swirling air.

She brought you here, drew you into her web. Other men have been trapped in it. She seeks to possess you, body and soul. Who will you be when she's done with you?

Cal all but fell into the door, panicked for a shuddering instant when he thought it locked. But his slippery hands yanked it open and he stumbled into the cool, sun-washed air of the bedroom. Behind him the mists swirled dark, shimmered greedily, then vanished.

What the hell? He found himself trembling all over, like a schoolboy rushing out of a haunted house. It had seemed as if there had been . . . something, something cold and slick and smelling of death crowded into that room with him, hiding in the mists.

But when Cal turned and stepped back to the door, he saw only a charming room, a fogged mirror, and the thinning steam from his shower.

Imagination working overtime, he thought, then let out half a laugh. Whose wouldn't, under the circumstances? But he shut the bathroom door firmly before he dressed and went down to find her.

She was spinning wool. Humming along with the quiet, rhythmic clacking of spindle and wheel. Her hands were as graceful as a harpist's on strings and her wool was as white as innocence.

Her dress was blue this morning, deep as her eyes. A thick silver chain carrying an ornately carved pendant hung between her breasts. Her hair was pinned up, leaving that porcelain face unframed.

Cal's hands itched for his camera. And for her.

She looked up, her hands never faltering, and smiled. "Well, did you decide to join the living, then?"

"My body clock's still in the States. Is it late?"

"Hmm, nearly half-ten. You'll be hungry, I'll wager. Come, have your coffee. I'll fix your breakfast."

He caught her hand as she rose. "You don't have to cook for me."

She laughed, kissed him lightly. "Oh, we'd have trouble soon enough if you thought I did. As it happens, it's my pleasure to cook for you this morning."

His eyes gleamed as he nibbled on her knuckles. "A full Irish breakfast? The works."

"If you like."

"Now that you mention it . . . ." His voice trailed off as he took a long, thorough study of her face. Her eyes were shadowed, her skin paler than it should have been. "You look tired. You didn't sleep well."

She only smiled and led him into the kitchen. "Maybe you snore."

"I do not." He nipped her at the waist, spun her around and kissed her. "Take it back."

"I only said maybe." Her brows shot up when his hands roamed around, cupped her bottom. "Are you always so frisky of a morning?"

"Maybe. I'll be friskier after I've had that coffee." He gave her a quick kiss before turning to pour himself a cup. "You know I noticed things this morning that I was too . . . distracted to take in yesterday. You don't have a phone."

She put a cast-iron skillet on a burner. "I have ways of calling those I need to call."

"Ah." He rubbed the chin he had neglected to shave. "Your kitchen's equipped with very modern appliances."

"If I choose to cook why would I use a campfire?" She sliced thick Irish bacon and put it on to sizzle and snap.

"Good point. You're out of sugar," he said absently when he lifted the lid on the bowl. "You spin your own wool, but you have a state-of-the-art stereo."

"Music is a comfort," she murmured, watching him go

unerringly to the pantry and fetch the unmarked tin that held her sugar supply.

"You make your own potions, but you buy your staples at the market." With quick efficiency, he filled her sugar bowl. "The contrast is fascinating. I wonder . . ." He stopped, stood with the sugar scoop in his hand, staring. "I knew where to find this," he said quietly. "I knew the sugar was on the second shelf in the white tin. The flour's in the blue one beside it. I knew that."

" 'Tis a gift. You've only forgotten to block it out. It shouldn't disturb you."

"Shouldn't disturb me." He neglected to add the sugar and drank his coffee black and bitter.

"It's yours to control, Cal, or to abjure."

"So if I don't want it, I can reject it."

"You've done so for half your life already."

It was her tone, bitter as the coffee, that had his eyes narrowing. "That annoys you."

She cut potatoes into quick slices, slid them into hot oil. "It's your choice."

"But it annoys you."

"All right, it does. You turn your back on it because you find it uncomfortable. Because it disturbs your sense of normality. As I do." She kept her back to him as she took the bacon out of the pan, set it to drain, picked up eggs. "You shut out your gift and me along with it because we didn't fit into your world. A tidy world where magic is only an illusion done with smoke and mirrors, where witches wear black hats, ride broomsticks, and cackle on All Hallows' Eve."

As the eggs cooked, she spooned up porridge, plopped the bowl on the table, and went back to slice bread. "A world where I have no place."

"I'm here, aren't I?" Cal said evenly. "Did I choose to be, Bryna, or did you will it?"

She uses you. She's drawn you into her web.

"Will it?" Insulted, struck to the bone, she whirled around to face him. "Is that what you think? After all I've told you, after all we've shared?"

"If I accept even half of what you've told me, if I put

aside logic and my own sense of reality and accept that I'm standing in the kitchen with a witch, a stone's throw away from an enchanted castle, about to do battle of some kind with an evil wizard in a war that has lasted a millennium, I think it's a remarkably reasonable question.''

"Reasonable?" With clenched teeth she swept back to the stove and shoveled eggs onto a platter. " 'It's reasonable,' says he. Have I pulled him in like a spider does a fly, lured him across an ocean and into my lair?'' She thumped the laden platter down and glared at him. "For what, might I ask you, Calin Farrell? For a fine bout of sex, for the amusement of having a man for a night or two. Well, I needn't have gone to such trouble for that. There's men enough in Ireland. Eat your breakfast or you'll be wearing it on your head like a hat."

Another time he might have smiled, but that sly voice was muttering in his ear. Still he sat, picked up his fork, tapped it idly against the plate. "You didn't answer the question. If I'm to believe you can't lie to me, isn't it odd that you've circled around the question and avoided a direct answer? Yes or no, Bryna. Did you will me here?''

"Yes or no?''

Her eyes were burning-dry, though her heart was weeping. Did he know he was looking at her with such doubt, such suspicion, such cool dispassion? There was no faith in the look, and none of the love she needed.

One night, she thought on a stab of despair, had not been enough.

"No, Calin, will you here I did not. If that had been my purpose, or in my power, would I have waited so long and so lonely for you? I asked you to come, begged without pride, for I needed you. But the choice to come or not was yours.''

She turned away, gripping the counter as she looked out the window toward the sea. "I'll give you more," she said quietly, "as time is short." She inhaled deeply. "You broke my heart when you shut me out of yours. Broke it to pieces, and it's taken me years to mend it as best I could. That choice was yours as well, for the knowledge was there in your head, and again in your heart if you chose to see it. All the answers are there, and you have only to look.''

''I want to hear them from you.''

She squeezed her eyes tightly shut. ''There are some I can't tell you, that you must find for yourself.'' She opened her eyes again, lifted her chin and turned back to him.

Her face was still pale, he noted, her eyes too dark. The hair she'd bundled up was slipping its pins, and her shoulders were stiff and straight.

''But there's something that's mine to tell, and I'll give you that. I was born loving you. There's been no other in my heart, even when you turned from me. Everything I am, or was, or will be, is yours. I cannot change my heart. I was born loving you,'' she said again. ''And I will die loving you. There is no choice for me.''

Turning, she bolted from the room.

CHAPTER 8

She'd vanished. Cal went after her almost immediately but found no trace. He rushed through the house, flinging open doors, calling her. Then cursing her.

Damn temperamental female, he decided. The fury spread through him. That she would tell him she loved him, then leave him before he had even a moment to examine his own heart!

She expected too much, he thought angrily. Wanted too much. Assumed too much.

He hurried out of the house, raced for the cliffs. But he didn't find her standing out on the rocks, staring out to sea with the wind billowing her hair. His voice echoed back to him emptily, infuriating him.

Then he turned, stared at the scarred stone walls of the castle. And knew. "All right, damn it," he muttered as he strode toward the ruins. "We're going to talk this through, straight. No magic, no legends, no bullshit. Just you and me."

He stepped toward the arch and bumped into air that had gone solid. Stunned, he reached out, felt the shield he couldn't see. He could see through it to the stony ground, the fire-scored walls, the tumble of rock, but the clear wall that blocked him was cold and solid.

"What kind of game is this?" Eyes narrowed, he drove his shoulder against it, yielded nothing. Snarling, he circled the walls, testing each opening, finding each blocked.

"Bryna!" He pounded the solidified air with his fists until

they ached. "Let me in. Goddamn it, let me pass!"

From the topmost turret, Bryna faced the sea. She heard him call for her, curse her. And oh, she wanted to answer. But her pride was scored, her power teetering.

And her decision made.

Perhaps she had made it during the sleepless night, curled against him, listening to him dream. Perhaps it had been made for her, eons before. She had been given only one single day with him, one single night. She knew, accepted, that if she'd been given more she might have broken her faith, let her fears and needs tumble out into his hands.

She couldn't tell him that her life, even her soul, was lost if by the hour of midnight his heart remained unsettled toward her. Unless he vowed his love, accepted it without question, there was no hope.

She had done all she could. Bryna turned her face to the wind, let it dry the tears that she was ashamed to have shed. Her charge would be protected, her lover spared, and the secrets of this place would die with her.

For Alasdair didn't know how strong was her will. Didn't know that in the amulet she wore around her neck was a powder of poison. If she should fail, and her love not triumph, then she would end her life before she faced one of bondage.

With Cal's voice battering the air, she closed her eyes, lifted her arms. She had only hours now to gather her forces.

She began the chant.

Hundreds of feet below, Cal backed away, panting. What the hell was he doing? he asked himself. Beating his head against a magic wall to get to a witch.

How had his life become a fairy tale?

Fairy tale or not, one thing was solid fact. Tick a woman off, and she sulks.

"Go on and sulk, then," he shouted. "When you're ready to talk like civilized people, let me know." His mood black, he stalked back to the house. He needed to get out, he told himself. To lose himself in work for a while, to let both of them cool off.

One day, he fumed. He'd had one day and she expected him to turn his life around. Pledge his undying love. The hell with that. She wasn't pushing him into anything he wasn't ready for. She could take her thousand-year-old spell and stuff it. He was a normal human being, and normal human beings didn't go riding off into the sunset with witches at the drop of a hat.

He shoved open the bedroom door, reached for his camera. Under it, folded neatly, was a gray sweater. He pulled his hand back and stared.

"That wasn't there an hour ago," he muttered. "Damn it, that wasn't there."

Gingerly he rubbed the material. Soft as a cloud, the color of storms. He remembered vaguely something about a cloak and a charm and wondered if this was Bryna's modern-day equivalent.

With a shrug, he peeled off his shirt and tried the sweater on. It fit as though it had been made for him. Of course it had, he realized. She'd spun the wool, dyed it, woven it. She'd known the length of his arms, the width of his chest. She'd known everything about him.

He was tempted to yank it off, toss it aside. He was tired of his life and his mind being open to her when so much of hers was closed to him.

But as he started to remove the sweater, he thought he heard her voice, whispering.

A gift. Only a gift.

He lifted his head, looked into the mirror. His face was unshaven, his hair wild, his eyes reflecting the storm-cloud color of the sweater.

"The hell with it," he muttered, and snatching up his camera and case, he left the house.

He wandered the hills for an hour, ran through roll after roll of film. Mockingbirds sang as he clambered over stone walls into fields where cows grazed on grass as green as emeralds. He saw farmers on tractors, tending their land under a cloud-thickened sky. Clothes flapping with whip snaps on the line, cats dozing in dooryards and sunbeams.

He wandered down a narrow dirt road where the hedgerows grew tall and thick. Through small breaks he spotted sumptuous gardens with flowers in rainbows of achingly beautiful colors. A woman with a straw hat over her red hair knelt by a flower bed, tugging up weeds and singing of a soldier gone to war. She smiled at him, lifted her hand in a wave as he passed by.

He wandered near a small wood, where leaves unfurled to welcome summer and a brook bubbled busily. The sun was straight up, the shadows short. Spending the morning in normal pursuits had settled his mood. He thought it was time to go back, see if Bryna had cooled down—perhaps try out the darkroom she had equipped.

A flash of white caught his eye, and he turned, then stared awestruck. A huge white stag stood at the edge of the leafy shadows, its blue eyes proud and wise.

Keeping his movements slow, controlled, Cal raised his camera, then swore lightly when the stag lifted his massive head, whirled with impossible speed and grace, and bounded into the trees.

"No, uh-uh, I'm not missing that." With a quick glance at the ruins, which he had kept always just in sight, Cal dived into the woods.

He had hunted wildlife with his camera before, knew how to move quietly and swiftly. He followed the sounds of the stag crashing through brush. A bird darted by, a black bullet with a ringed neck, as Cal leaped over the narrow brook, skidded on the damp bank, and dug in for the chase.

Sun dappled through the leaves, dazzling his eyes, and sweat rolled down his back. Annoyed, he pushed the arms of the sweater up to his elbows and strained to listen.

Now there was silence, complete and absolute. No breeze stirred, no bird sang. Frustrated, he shoved the hair out of his eyes, his breath becoming labored in the sudden stifling heat. His throat was parchment-dry, and thinking of the cold, clear water of the brook, he backtracked.

The sun burned like a furnace through the sheltering leaves now. It surprised him that they didn't singe and curl under the onslaught. Desperate for relief, he pulled off the sweater, laid it on the ground beside him as he knelt by the brook.

He reached down to cup water in his hand. And pulled back a cup of coffee.

"Do you good to get away for a few days, change of scene."

"What?" He stared down at the mug in his hand, then looked up into his mother's concerned face.

"Honey, are you all right? You've gone pale. Come sit down."

"I . . . Mom?"

"Here, now, he needs some water, not caffeine." Cal saw his father set down his fishing flies and rise quickly. Water ran out of the kitchen faucet into a glass. "Too much caffeine, if you ask me. Too many late nights in the darkroom. You're wearing yourself out, Cal."

He sipped water, tasted it. Shuddered. "I—I had a dream."

"That's all right." Sylvia rubbed his shoulders. "Everybody has dreams. Don't worry. Don't think about them. We don't want you to think about them."

"No—I thought it was, it wasn't . . ." Wasn't like before? he thought. It was more than before. "I went to Ireland." He took a deep breath, tried to clear his hazy brain. Desperately, he wanted to turn, rest his head against his mother's breast like a child. "Did I go to Ireland?"

"You haven't been out of New York in the last two months, slaving to get that exhibition ready." His father's brow creased. Cal saw the worry in his eyes, that old baffled look of concern. "You need a rest, boy."

"I'm not going crazy."

"Of course you're not." Sylvia murmured it, but Cal caught the faint uncertainty in her voice. "You're just imagining things."

"No, it's too real." He took his mother's hand, gripped it hard. He needed her to believe him, to trust him. "There's a woman. Bryna."

"You've got a new girl and didn't tell us." Sylvia clucked her tongue. "That's what this is about?"

Was that relief in her voice, Cal wondered, or doubt?

"Bryna—that's an odd name, isn't it, John? Pretty, though, and old-fashioned."

"She's a witch."

John chuckled heartily. "They all are, son. Each and every one." John picked up one of his fishing lures. The black fly fluttered in his fingers, its wings desperate for freedom. "Don't you worry now."

"I—I need to get back."

"You need to sleep," John said, toying with the fly. "Sleep and don't give her a thought. One woman's the same as another. She's only trying to trap you. Remember?"

"No." The fly, alive in his father's fingers. No, no, not his father's hand. Too narrow, too long. His father had work-ingman's hands, calloused, honest. "No," Cal said again, and as he scraped back his chair, he saw cold fury light his father's eyes.

"Sit down."

"The hell with you."

"Calin! Don't you speak to your father in that tone."

His mother's voice was a shriek—a hawk's call to prey—cutting through his head. "You're not real." He was suddenly calm, deadly calm. "I reject you."

He was running down a narrow road where the hedgerows towered and pressed close. He was breathless, his heart hammering. His eyes were focused on the ruined walls of the castle high on the cliff—and too far away.

"Bryna."

"She waits for you." The woman with the straw hat over her red hair looked up from her weeding and smiled sadly. "She always has, and always will."

His side burned from cramping muscles. Gasping for air, Cal pressed a hand against the pain. "Who are you?"

"She has a mother who loves her, a father who fears for her. Do you think that those who hold magic need family less than you? Have hearts less fragile? Needs less great?"

With a weary sigh, she rose, walked toward him and stepped into the break in the hedge. Her eyes were green, he saw, and filled with worry, but the mouth with its serious smile was Bryna's.

"You question what she is—and what she is bars you from giving your heart freely. Knowing this, and loving you, she has sent you away from danger and faces the night alone."

"Sent me where? How? Who are you?"

"She's my child," the woman said, "and I am helpless." The smile curved a little wider. "Almost helpless. Look to the clearing, Calin Farrell, and take what is offered to you. My daughter waits. Without you, she dies this night."

"Dies?" Terror gripped his belly. "Am I too late?"

She only shook her head and faded back into air.

He awoke, drenched with sweat, stretched out on the cool, damp grass of the bank. And the moon was rising in a dark sky.

"No." He stumbled to his feet, found the sweater clutched in his hand. "I won't be too late. I can't be too late." He dragged the sweater over his head as he ran.

Now the trees lashed, whipped by a wind that came from nowhere and howled like a man gone mad. They slashed at him, twined together like mesh to block his path with gnarled branches armed with thorns. He fought his way through, ignored the gash that sliced through denim into flesh.

Overhead, lighting cut like a broadsword and dimmed the glow of the full white moon.

Alasdair. Hate roiled up inside him, fighting against the love he'd only just discovered. Alasdair would not win, if he had to die to prevent it.

"Bryna." He lifted his head to the sky as it exploded with wild, furious rain. "Wait for me. I love you."

The stag stood before him, white as bone, its patient eyes focused. Cal rushed forward as it turned and leaped into the shadows. With only instinct to trust, he plunged into the dark to follow the trail. The ground trembled under his feet, thorns ripped his clothes to tatters as he raced to keep that flash of white in sight.

Then it was gone as he fell bleeding into a clearing where moonlight fought through the clouds to beam on a jet-black horse.

Without hesitation, Calin accepted the impossible. Taking

the reins, he vaulted into the saddle, his knees vising as the stallion reared and trumpeted a battle cry. As he rode, he heard the snap of a cloak flying and felt the hilt of a sword gripped in his own hand.

CHAPTER 9

The Castle of Secrets glimmered with the light of a thousand torches. Its walls glinted silver and speared up toward the moon. The stone floor of the great hall was smooth as marble. In the center of the charmed circle cast by the ancients, Bryna stood in a robe of white, her hair a fall of fire, her eyes the blue of heated steel.

Here she would make her stand.

"Do you call the thunder and whistle up the winds, Alasdair? Such showmanship."

In a swirl of smoke, a sting of sulphur, he appeared before her. Solid now, his flesh as real as hers. He wore the robes of crimson, of blood and power. His golden looks were beautiful, an angel's face but for the contrast of those dark, damning eyes.

"And an impressive, if overdone entrance," Bryna said lightly, though her pulse shuddered.

"Your trouble, my darling, is that you fail to appreciate the true delights of power. Contenting yourself with your woman's charms and potions when worlds are at your mercy."

"I take my oath, and my gifts, to heart, Alasdair. Unlike you."

"My only oath is to myself. You'll belong to me, Bryna, body and soul. And you will give me what I want the most." He flung up a hand so that the walls shook. "Where is the globe?"

"Beyond you, Alasdair, where it will remain. As I will."

She gestured sharply, shot a bolt of white light into the air to land and burn at his feet. A foolish gesture, she knew, but she needed to impress him.

He angled his head, smiled indulgently. "Pretty tricks. The moon is rising to midnight, Bryna. The time of waiting is ending. Your warrior has deserted you once again."

He stepped closer, careful not to test the edge of the circle and his voice became soft, seductive. "Why not accept—even embrace—what I offer you? Lifetimes of power and pleasure. Riches beyond imagination. You have only to accept, to take my hand, and we will rule together."

"I want no part of your kingdom, and I would rather be bedded by a snake than have your hands on me."

Murky blue fire gleamed at his fingertips, his anger taking form. "You've felt them on you in your dreams. And you'll feel them again. Gentle I can be, or punishing, but you'll never feel another's hand but mine. He's lost to you, Bryna. And you are lost to me."

"He's safe from you." She threw up her head. "So I have already won." Lifting her hands, she loosed a whip of power, sent him flying back. "Be gone from this place." Her voice filled the great hall, rang like bells. "Or face the death of mortals."

He wiped a hand over his mouth, furious that she'd drawn first blood. "A battle, then."

At his vicious cry, a shadow formed at his feet, and the shadow took the shape of a wolf, black-pelted, red-eyed, fangs bared. With a snarl, it sprang, leaping toward Bryna's throat.

Cal pounded up the cliff, driving his mount furiously. The castle glowed brilliant with light, its walls tall and solid again, its turrets shafts of silver that nicked the cloud-chased moon. With a burst of knowledge, he thrust a hand inside the cloak and drew out the globe that waited there.

It swam red as blood, fire sparks of light piercing the clouds. He willed them to clear, willed himself to see as he thundered higher toward the crest of the cliff.

Visions came quickly, overlapping, rushing. Bryna weep-

ing as she watched him sleep. The dark chamber with the
globe held between them and her whispering her spell.

*You will be safe, you will be free. There is nothing, my
love, you cannot ask of me. Follow the stag whose pelt is
white, if your heart is not open come not back in the night.
This gift and this duty I trust unto you. The globe of hope
and visions true. Live, and be well, and remember me not.
What cannot be held is best forgot. What I do I do free. As
I will, so mote it be.*

And terror struck like a snake, its fangs plunging deep into
the heart. For he knew what she meant to do.

She meant to die.

She wanted to live, and fought fiercely. She sliced the wolf,
cleaving its head from its body with one stroke of will. And
its blood was black.

She sent her lights blazing, the burning cold that would
scorch the flesh and freeze the bone.

And knew she would lose when midnight rang.

Alasdair's robes smoked from the violence of her power.
And still he could not break the circle and claim her.

He sent the ground heaving under her feet, watched her
sway, then fall to her knees. And his smile bloomed dark
when her head fell weakly and that fiery curtain of hair rained
over the shuddering stones.

"Will you ask for pain, Bryna?" He stepped closer, felt
the hot licks when his soft boots skimmed the verge of the
circle. Not yet, he warned himself, inching back. But soon.
Her spell was waning. "Just take my hand, spare yourself.
We will forget this battle and rule. Give me your hand, and
give me the globe."

Her breath was short and shallow. She whispered words
in the old tongue, the secrets of magic, incantations that flickered weakly as her power slipped like water through her fingers.

"I will not yield."

"You will." He inched closer again, pleased when he met
with only faint resistance. "You have no choice. The charm
was cast, the time has come. You belong to me now."

He reached down, and her shoulder burned where his fingers brushed. "I belong to Calin." She gripped the amulet, steeling herself, then flipped its poison chamber open with her thumb. She whipped her head up and, with a last show of defiance, smiled. "You will never have what is his."

She brought the amulet to her lips, prepared to take the powder.

The horse and rider burst into the torchlight in a flurry of black, storm-gray, and bright steel.

"Would you rather die than trust me?" Cal demanded furiously.

The amulet slipped through her fingers, the powder sifted onto the stones. "Calin."

"Touch her, Alasdair"—Cal controlled the restless horse as if he'd been born astride one—"and I'll cut off your hands at the wrists."

Though there was alarm, and there was shock, Alasdair straightened slowly. He would not lose now. The woman was already defeated, he calculated, and the man was, after all, only a foolish mortal. "You were a warrior a thousand years ago, Caelan of Farrell. You are no warrior tonight."

Cal vaulted from the horse, and his sword sang as he pulled it from its scabbard. "Try me."

Unexpected little flicks of fear twisted in Alasdair's belly. But he circled his opponent, already plotting. "I will bring such fury raining down on your head . . ." He crossed his arms over his chest, then flung them to the side. Black balls of lightning shot out, hissing trails of snaking sparks.

Instinctively Cal raised the sword. Pain and power shot up his arm as the charges struck, careened away, and crashed smoking into stone.

"Do you think such pitiful weapons can defend against a power such as mine?" Arrogance and rage rang in Alasdair's voice as he hurled arrows of flame. His cry echoed monstrously as the arrows struck Cal's cloak and melted into water.

"Your power is nothing here."

Bryna was on her feet again, her white robe swirling like

foam. And her face so glowed with beauty that both men stared in wonder.

"I am the guardian of this place." Her voice was deeper, fuller, as if a thousand voices joined it. "I am a witch whose power flows clean. I am a woman whose heart is bespoken. I am the keeper of all you will never own. Fear me, Alasdair. And fear the warrior who stands with me."

"He will not stand with you. And what you guard, I will destroy." With fists clenched, he called the flames, shot the torches from their homes to wheel and burn and scorch the air. "You will bow yet to my will."

With lifted arms, Bryna brought the rain, streaming pure and cool through the flames to douse them. And felt as the damp air swirled, the power pour through her, from her, as rich and potent as any she'd known.

"Save this place," Alasdair warned, "and lose the man." He whirled on Cal, sneered at the lifted sword. "Remember death."

Like a blade sliced through the belly, the agony struck. Blood flowed through his numbed fingers, and the sword clattered onto the wet stone. He saw his death, leaping like a beast, and heard Bryna's scream of fear and rage.

"You will not harm him. It's trickery only, Calin, hear me." But her terror for him was so blinding that she ran to him, leaving the charm of the circle.

The bolt of energy slapped her like a jagged fist, sent her reeling, crumbling. Paralyzed, she fought for her strength but found the power that had flowed so pure and true now only an ebbing flicker.

"Calin." The hand she'd flung out to shield him refused to move. She could only watch as he knelt on the stones, unarmed, bleeding, beyond her reach. "You must believe," she whispered. "Trust. Believe or all is lost."

"He loses faith, you lose your power." Robes singed and smoking, Alasdair stood over her. "He is weak and blind, and you have proven yourself more woman than witch to trade your power for his life."

Reaching down, he grabbed her hair and dragged her roughly to her knees. "You have nothing left," he said to her. "Give me the globe, come to me freely, and I will spare you from pain."

"You will have neither." She gripped the amulet, despairing that its chamber was empty. She bit off a cry as icy fingers squeezed viciously around her heart.

"From this time and this place, you are in bondage to me for a hundred years times ten. And this pain you feel will be yours to keep until you bend your will to mine."

He lowered his gaze to her mouth. "A kiss," he said, "to seal the spell."

She was wrenched out of his arms, her fingers locked with Cal's. Even as she whispered his name, he stepped in front of her, raised the sword in both hands so that it shimmered silver and sharp.

"Your day is done." Cal's eyes burned and the pain swirling through him only added to his strength. "Can you bleed, wizard?" he demanded and brought the sword down like fury.

There was a cry, ululating, inhuman, a stench of sulphur, a blinding flash. The ground heaved, the stones shook, and lightning, cold and blue, speared out of the air and struck.

The explosion lifted him off his feet. Even as he grabbed for Bryna, Cal felt the hot, greedy hand of it hurl him into the whirling air, into the dark.

CHAPTER 10

Visions played through his head. Too many to count. Voices hummed and murmured. Women wept. Charms were chanted. He swam through them, weighed down with weariness.

Someone told him to sleep, to be easy, but he shook off the words and the phantom hands that stroked his brow.

He had slept long enough.

He came to, groggy, aching in every bone. The thin light of pre-dawn filtered the air. He thought he heard whispering, but decided it was just the beat of the sea and the flow of the wind through grass.

He could see the last of the stars just winking out. And with a moan, he turned his head and tried to shake off the dream.

The cat was watching him, sitting patiently, her eyes unblinking. Dazed, he pushed himself up on his elbows, wincing from the pain, and saw that he was lying on the ground outside the ruins.

Gone were the tall silver spears, the glowing torches that had lighted the great hall. It was, as it had been when he'd first seen it, a remnant of what it once had been, a place where the wind wound about and the grass and wildflowers forced their way through stony ground.

But the scent of smoke and blood still stung the air.

"Bryna." Panicked, he heaved himself to his feet. And nearly stumbled over her.

She was sprawled on the ground, one arm outflung. Her

face was pale, bruised, her white robe torn and scorched. He fell to his knees, terrified that he would find no pulse, no spark of life. But he found it, beating in her throat, and shuddering with relief, he lowered his lips to hers.

"Bryna," he said again. "Bryna."

She stirred, her lashes fluttering, her lips moving against his. "Calin. You came back. You fought for me."

"You should have known I would." He lifted her so that he could cradle her against him, resting a cheek on her hair. "How could you have kept it from me? How could you have sent me away?"

"I did what I thought best. When it came to facing it, I couldn't risk you."

"He hurt you." He squeezed his eyes tight as he remembered how she'd leaped from safety and been struck down.

"Small hurts, soon over." She turned, laid her hands on his face. There were bruises there as well, cuts and burns. "Here." Gently, she passed her hands over them, took them away. Her face knit in concentration, she knelt and stroked her fingers over his body, skimming where the cloak hadn't shielded until every wound was gone. "There. No pain," she murmured. "No more."

"You're hurt." He lifted her as he rose.

"It's a different matter to heal oneself. I have what I need in the cupboard, in the kitchen."

"We weren't alone here. After?"

"No." Oh, she was so weary, so very weary. "Family watches over. The white bottle," she told him as he carried her through the kitchen door and sat her at the table. "The square one, and the small green one with the round stopper."

"You have explaining to do, Bryna." He set the bottles on the table, fetched her a glass. "When you're stronger."

"Yes, we've things to discuss." With an expert hand, an experienced eye, she mixed the potions into the glass, let them swirl and merge until the liquid went clear as plain water. "But would you mind, Calin, I'd like a bath and a change of clothes first."

"Conjure it," he snapped. "I want this settled."

"I would do that, but I prefer the indulgence. I'll ask you

for an hour." She rose, cupping the glass in both hands. "It's only an hour, Calin, after all."

"One thing." He put a hand on her arm. "You told me you couldn't lie to me, that it was forbidden."

"And never did I lie to you. But I came close to the line with omission. One hour," she said on a sigh that weakened him. "Please."

He let her go and tried to soothe his impatience by brewing tea. His cloak was gone, he noted, and the sweater she'd woven for him stank of smoke and blood. He stripped it off, tossed it over the back of a chair, then glanced down as the cat came slinking into the room.

"So how do I handle her now?" Cal cocked his head, studied those bland blue eyes. "Any suggestions? You'd be her familiar, wouldn't you? Just how familiar are you?"

Content with the cat for company, he crouched down and stroked the silky black fur. "Are you a shape-shifter too?" He tilted the cat's head up with a finger under the chin. "Those eyes looked at me from out of the face of a white stag."

Letting out a breath, he simply sat on the floor, let the cat step into his lap and knead. "Let me tell you something, Hecate. If a two-headed dragon walked up and knocked on the kitchen door, I wouldn't blink an eye. Nothing is ever going to surprise me again."

But he was wrong about that. He was stunned with surprise when Bryna came downstairs again. She was as he'd seen her the night before, when her power had glowed in her face, striking it with impossible beauty.

"You were beautiful before," he managed, "but now . . . Is this real?"

"Everything's real." She smiled, took his hand. "Would you walk with me, Cal? I'm wanting the air and the sun."

"I have questions, Bryna."

"I know it," she said as they stepped outside. Her body felt light again, free of aches. Her mind was clear. "You're angry because you feel I deceived you, but it wasn't deception."

"You sent the white stag to lure me into the woods, away from you."

"I did, yes. I see now that Alasdair knew, and he used it against me. I wanted you safe. Knowing you now—the man you are now—that became more important than . . ." She looked at the castle. "Than the rest. But he tricked you into removing the protection I'd given you, then sent you into dreams to cloud your mind and make you doubt your reason."

"There was a woman . . . she said she was your mother."

"My mother." Bryna blinked once, then her lips curved. "Was she in her garden, wearing a foolish hat of straw?"

"Yes, and she had your mouth and hair."

Clucking her tongue, Bryna strolled toward the ruins. "She wasn't meant to interfere. But perhaps it was permitted, as I bent the rules a bit myself. The air's clearing of him," she added as she stepped under the arch. "The flowers still bloom here."

He saw the circle of flowers, untouched, unscarred. "It's over, then. Completely?"

Completely, she thought and fought to keep her smile in place. "He's destroyed. Even at the moment of his destruction he tried to take us with him. He might have done it if you hadn't been quick, if you hadn't been willing to risk."

"Where's the globe now?"

"You know where it is. And there it stays. Safe."

"You trusted me with that, but you didn't trust me with you."

"No." She looked down at the hands she'd linked together. "That was wrong of me."

"You were going to take poison."

She bit her lip at the raw accusation in his voice. "I couldn't face what he had in mind for me. I couldn't bear it, however weak it makes me. I couldn't bear it."

"If I'd been a moment later, you would have done it. Killed yourself. Killed yourself," he repeated, jerking her head up. "You couldn't trust me to help you."

"No, I was afraid to. I was afraid and hurt and desperate.

Have I not the right to feelings? Do you think what I am strips me of them?''

Her mother had asked almost the same of him, he remembered. "No." He said it very calmly, very clearly. "I don't. Do you think what I'm not makes me less?''

Stunned, she shook her head, and pressing a hand to her lips, turned away. It wasn't only he who had questioned, she realized. Not only he who had lacked faith.

"I've been unfair to you, and I'm sorry for it. You came here for me and learned to accept the impossible in only one day.''

"Because part of me accepted it all along. Burying something doesn't mean it ceases to exist. We were born for what happened here." He let out an impatient breath. Why were her shoulders slumped, he wondered, when the worse of any life was behind them? "We've done what we were meant to do, and maybe it was done as it was meant to be.''

"You're right, of course." Her shoulders straightened as she turned, and her smile was bright. And false, he realized as he looked into her eyes.

"He can't come back and touch you now.''

"No." She shook her head, laid a hand briefly on his. "Nor you. He was swallowed by his own. His kind are always here, but Alasdair is no more.''

Then with a laugh she brought his hand to her cheek. "Oh, Cal, if I could give you a picture, as fine and bold as any of your own. How you looked when you hefted that sword over your head, the light in your eyes, the strength rippling in waves around you. I'll carry that with me, always.''

She turned then, walked regally to the circle of flowers. In the center she turned, faced him, held out her hands. "Calin Farrell, you met your fate. You came to me when my need was great, when my life was imperiled. In this place you stood between me and the unbearable, fought against magic dark and deadly, wielded sword for me. You've saved my life and in so doing saved this place and all I guard in it.''

"Quite a speech," he murmured and stepped closer.

She only smiled. "You're brave and true of heart. And from this hour, from this place you are free.''

"Free?" Understanding was dawning, and he angled his head. "Free from you, Bryna?"

"Free from all and ever. The spell is broken, and you have no debt to pay. But a debt is owed. Whatever you ask that is in my power you shall have. Whatever boon you wish will be yours."

"A boon, is it?" He tucked his tongue in his cheek. "Oh, let's say, like immortality?"

Her eyes flickered—disappointment quickly masked. "Such things aren't within the power I hold."

"Too tough for you, huh?" With a nod, he circled around her as if considering. "But if I decided on, say, unlimited wealth or incredible sexual powers, you could handle that."

Her chin shot up another inch, went rigid. "I could, if it's what you will. But a warning before you choose. Be wary and sure of what you wish for. Every gift, even given freely, has a price."

"Yeah, yeah. I've heard that. Let's think about it. Money? Sex? Power, maybe. Power's good. I could have a nice island in the Caribbean, be a benign despot. I could get into that."

"This offer was not made for your amusement," she said stiffly.

"No? Well, it tickles the hell out of me." Rocking back on his heels, he tucked his hands into his pockets. "All I had to do was knock off an evil wizard and save the girl, and I can have whatever I want. Not a bad deal, all in all. So, just what do I want?"

He narrowed his eyes in consideration, then stepped into the circle. "You."

Eyes widening, she jerked back. "What?"

"You. I want you."

"To—to do what?" she said stupidly, then blinked when he roared with laughter. "Oh, you've no need to waste a boon there." She lifted her hands to unfasten her dress, and found them caught in his.

"That, too," he said, walking her backward out of the circle, keeping her arms up, her hands locked behind her head. "Yeah, in fact, I look forward to quite a bit of that."

The warrior was back, she thought dizzily. There, the glint

of battle and triumph in his eyes. "What are you doing?"

"I'm holding you to your boon. You, Bryna, all of you, no restrictions. For better or worse," he continued until he had her backed against the wall. "For richer or poorer. That's the deal."

She couldn't get her breath, couldn't keep her balance. "You want . . . me?"

"I'm not getting down on one knee when it's my boon."

"But you're free. The spell is broken. I have no hold on you."

"Don't you?" He lowered his mouth, buckling her knees with his kiss. "You can't lie to me." He crushed his lips to hers again, pulling her closer. "You were born loving me." He swallowed her moan and dived deeper. "You'll die loving me."

"Yes." Powerless, she flexed the hands he held above her head.

"Look at me," he murmured, easing back as she trembled. "And see." He gentled his hands, lowered them to stoke her shoulders. "Beautiful Bryna. Mine. Only mine."

"Calin." Her heart wheeled when his lips brushed tenderly over hers. "You love me. After it's done, after it's only you and only me. You love me."

"I was born loving you." The kiss was deep and sweet. "I'll die loving you." He sipped the tears from her cheeks.

"This is real," she said in a whisper. "This is true magic."

"It's real. Whatever came before, this is what's real. I love you, Bryna. You," he repeated. "The woman who puts whiskey in my tea, and the witch who weaves me magic sweaters. Believe that."

"I do." Her breath released on a shudder of joy. She felt it. Love. Trust. Acceptance. "I do believe it."

"It's time we made a home together, Bryna. We've waited long enough."

"Calin Farrell." She wound her arms around his neck, pressed her cheek against his. "Your boon is granted."

NORA ROBERTS

BLUE SMOKE

PUTNAM